Loving Kids Like Jesus
By: Alison Neihardt MA, LPC

Table of Contents

I would like to dedicate this book in loving memory of my grandma, Alice J. Babcock (1926-2019). She was the person who taught me what it meant to "Love Kids Like Jesus." She had 6 children, 34 grandchildren, and 42 great grandchildren. She worked as an aid in an emotionally impaired classroom for 16 years. She taught Sunday School at Kalkaska Church of Christ for 55 years. She made herself available to children just like Jesus did.

This was the last Vacation Bible School she helped with. (Photo Credit: Anita Severance)

Bio

Alison has always had a passion for working with children. This began when she was twelve years old with babysitting. She has taught in schools, daycares, in churches, and finally into counseling children, teens and their parents since 2008. She received her Master's degree from Spring Arbor University. She also earned under graduate degrees in Religious Education and Counseling from Great Lakes Christian College as well as an Associates in Early Childhood Education. All of this is applied to helping children and families daily in her private practice in Northern Michigan.

My Mission

Helping Kids is my calling not just the name of my business. I love children. I always have. I began babysitting at the age of twelve and have worked with children ever since. I love helping children and their families. This is my life work. I have worked at as a teacher, children's minister, missionary, Sunday School Teacher, Vacation Bible School Director, and now counselor.

I see hurting and struggling children and I just want to reach out and help. It could be a problem they are having at home; it could be someone is hurting them, or they are having a hard time in school. I just want to help them make it better.

In Sunday School class, every week I do a check in with my second and third graders. This allows them time to tell me what is going on in their lives. They know I will listen to them. They also know that I am interested in them. I still have kids after many years of teaching Sunday School who still come to me when they are having a problem or to just get a hug.

I get asked often if I have children. No, I do not, but the kids who come through my door whether in my office, or my Sunday School classroom are "my" kids. I do my best to look after them. That saying, "it takes a village" is so very true. My church parents know that if there is something serious going on with their kids and I find out about it that I will most definitely let them know!

Why am I telling all of this? For one it is what is on my heart, and for two I take the scripture of Jesus letting the little children come to Him very seriously. We need to be like Jesus and let the children come to us. We need to be approachable. Kids need to know they can come to us when they need help. They need to know they have grown-up friends who love them and care about them.

As adults, we need to invest in the lives of children on a daily basis. Whether as a parent, grandparent, aunt, uncle, or friend. Kids need to know they matter. We want children to be successful adults, so we adults need to help them.

Some kids go through so much, and they have a hard time trusting adults. We need to be an adult they can trust. We may be the only one. It is possible to overcome the hurt, pain and trauma that happens to kids, with the right people there helping. It needs to be our mission to invest in children in a positive way to help them become a successful adult.

Introduction

All of work, whether in the home or outside of the home, we take care of those around us. It doesn't matter if you are a stay at home mom, a teacher, a counselor, a volunteer at church, a pastor, or a cashier at the local grocery store, are you "loving kids like Jesus?"

When I say to love a child like Jesus did what do I mean? I have worked with children since I started baby sitting at the age of twelve. Over my years of experience in a variety of jobs and careers I have had I have learned one thing, kids are crazy!! To love a child like Jesus would is not an easy task. In the book of Matthew Jesus is telling his disciples to "Let the little children come to me, and do not hinder them, for the kingdom of heaven belongs to such as these." Jesus is telling them to not hinder the children to come to Him. Jesus wanted the children to know they are loved too. He wanted to make himself approachable.

What does "to be approachable" mean? It means children can come to you and feel safe, welcome and comfortable. In many aspects, children are left to the side and not taken seriously. They feel unheard. They feel like adults don't care about them. Children are hurting and feeling unloved in our world today.

We need to create an environment where children feel safe and cared for. In my counseling office it is very obvious I work with children. I have toys, games, stuffed animals, and other things kids find fun. I also have a snack bucket. If a child is hungry while talking to me, they can have a snack. I put things that are healthy and they like in the bucket. Because let's face it, it is really hard to talk to a hungry kid!

Jesus also tells us in Matthew "if we give a cup of cold water to one of these little ones because he is my disciple, I tell you the truth, he will certainly not lose his reward." It is our job as those who love and care for others to also love and care for children. They are our next generation. If we are to break the cycle of poverty and abuse in our world we need to step up and help the next generation.

How do we help the next generation be able to not only get by, but flourish? How do we help these children in practical ways? This is what I will be discussing throughout this book. I have worked with children and parents in many different ways and in many different settings. From local to foreign missions, churches, non-profits, teaching, and counseling.

I try to think outside the box when it comes to helping others. I try to be creative in my solutions and the ways I offer and extend help and services to those around me. I try to follow God's leading to know how He would want something done. I have gone out and purchased clothes for a child in need, school supplies, food, and other things. Sometimes it is just that kids need a hug because they have had a hard day.

Chapter 1—Kids and Feelings

Kids and Feelings

One of the first things I do when I begin counseling a child especially a young child is to help them label how they feel. We talk about feelings. We play games and read books about feelings. Children need to learn what feelings are and how to tell others how they feel.

The next thing I do is teach them what to do with their feelings. We also talk about who they can trust with their feelings. We talk about how the feelings feel in their bodies. Where they feel angry or sad. If they get headaches or stomach aches when they are worried or stressed.

When God created us, He made us to have feelings. He also wants us to be able to have self-control and awareness of what our feelings are and how they affect us. To be able to label feelings at a young age gives kids power to deal with them. Kids and adults both need to understand feelings are normal. God made us to have feelings.

Do children have feelings?

Well of course they do! But, sometimes as adults we do not recognize when a child is experiencing feelings, whether they are good feelings or negative feelings. Sometimes children can become pretty intense with their emotions. You know, they scream, yell, cry, throw themselves on the floor kicking and screaming in the middle of a store. The other side is they are excited and jumping up and down laughing and giggling.

It is always a good idea to acknowledge feelings. Something along the lines of "I see you are excited to go play," or "I see you are angry right now. What can I do to help?" If feelings are noticed and talked about kids will see they are accepted by you no matter the feeling they have.

In some cases, if a child or teen does not feel heard they will also shut down and let their feelings bottle up inside of themselves. This is not a good thing either for so many reasons. Children and teens begin to develop anxiety and depression. They also develop anger issues because they feel like they are not important or not allowed to express how they feel. They feel like their feelings are not important. So, they do not share their feelings with anyone. They then begin to do destructive things like self-harm, isolate, "act out," hurt others, and feel they are alone.

God gave us feelings. It is part of who we are as humans. We as adults need to help children recognize and label their feelings to help children better understand the emotions they have when they are having them. For example, a child is crying, we as an adult may say, "You look sad, is there something I can do to help?" Or, "You look angry, what is upsetting you?" I know this is easier said than done, especially when you as a parent are upset with your child because they have done something that upsets you.

However, that is part of the job of an adult is to help a child. This is may be where taking a break or time out so that YOU as the adult can get your emotions under control could be helpful. If the adult is just as upset and frustrated as the child then all that happens is emotional chaos. If we as adults can tell what our feelings are, we can help children label theirs. This is a key part in teaching children how to label their feelings and communication with not only you as a parent or adult, but also helps the child recognize that feelings and emotions can be controlled. It takes practice to be able to control feelings and emotions no one is perfect. This is part of learning self-control.

I tell the children I work with all the time that it is okay to be angry, however it is not okay do to something naughty (sin) in their anger. Children begin to recognize when they are mad. For some it takes longer than others. This is also helping children see that they can be heard and understood in their feelings and emotions and that we still accept them even when they are having negative emotions and love them anyway.

How do we as adults help children and teens with "big" emotions? Well, for starters, acknowledge when a child is feeling emotional. Some feelings are easier to deal with then others. Second, talk to your child or teen about what is bothering them. Maybe they are having a bad day. Maybe they got in trouble at school, or someone at school is picking on them. Keeping the lines of communication open is very important! Even when they are young children, they still have big feelings. Sometimes giving some space for children to think and get themselves under control also helps.

Are children still punished for "acting out?" Yes, children and teens need to know their limits and that is part of gaining control over their feelings. It is never okay for a child or teen to disrespect an adult. When this happens there needs to be some correction involved. If a child or teen is not corrected then they think that is it is acceptable to continue their behavior. For some children and teens this is a long process and, in many cases, needs to be repeated MANY times! Having consistency helps this process. Do not give up!

Overall, just be aware of the children and teen's emotional needs that are entrusted to your care. They look to adults to set the example and help with their problems even if they do not come out and ask, they still what guidance, direction, and limits!

Exploding Kids…What to do with a Kid with an Anger Problem.

Does your child stomp their feet? Slam doors in your house? Yell? Scream? Argue ALL THE TIME? Do they cry a lot? They are most likely angry about something. They easily lose their temper and yell or get upset for no apparent reason. You as a parent or caregiver get tired of the anger and then you get frustrated and angry too. Do you see the cycle?

How do we as adults help these exploding kids? First when they yell at you try not to yell back. Notice I said TRY. I know it is hard in the heat of the moment to not lose it and yell at your kid. It can turn into a shouting match of which no one wins! It just creates more anger and more frustration on both sides.

Try to separate yourself from your child and take a break and give them a break as well. Because, honestly, they are probably just as angry with you as you are with them. They may not really be angry with you. They may have had a bad day at school, they maybe have someone who is bullying them at school, and they may be really struggling with something you are not even aware of. They just know they are MAD!

Also, kids who go through change like a divorce, being placed in foster care, death, or some other crisis are actually mad about that verses actually being angry with you. You just happen to be standing there at the time. They are so deeply wounded that they do not know how to express themselves. They cannot be mad at the person who actually deserves it because they are not around. So, you are the lucky target.

How do we help these angry kids? First, we need to acknowledge that they are angry whether they realize it or not. Say something like, "I see that you are upset. Would you like to tell me about it?" Allow your child to be open with you; even if that means that they are mad at you! Maybe you hurt your child's feelings or did something that upset them, or they misunderstood something.

Second, if the anger is a "big" issue and the anger is not going away then your child most likely needs a professional to help them and you with their anger. Please seek this help for your child! They will thank you for it later.

Third, help your child identify how to know when they are getting angry. Signs might include, stomping feet, slamming doors, yelling, crying, pouting, shutting down, mean looks, and the list goes on! You know our child and what they do!

Helping an angry child is not easy. You need to set limits and not allow them to do something out of anger that will cause themselves or someone else, including you harm. When kids get angry, they are not rational. Their emotions are running so high that they do not know what they are doing or saying. They may not even remember what they say or what you say.

It is better to save your conversation or lecture for when they are calm and can talk rationally. Yes, this may take time. This is why a time out or a break is important for both of you. Also, remember when you are talking with your child to talk in a way that is appropriate for their age. When you talk for a long period of time your child will tune you out and not listen. Make your conversations as short as possible.

Also, when they do something out of anger that does harm someone else or property then yes there needs to be consequences to those things. Whatever is appropriate, an apology, fixing or replacing what they broke, cleaning up the mess they made, etc.

Having a child who is angry is not easy. It can be frustrating and exhausting. But, just remember what has gotten them to the point of being so angry and help them deal with it in a healthy way. It is okay to show anger, just not to do harm in the process. If your child needs to do something physical to get rid of the angry feelings, then have let then bounce a ball, run, jump, ride their bike.

If they need space to process their feelings quietly give them some space. Some kids can write or draw about how they feel. Giving them tools to help with the anger can help when the anger comes. Make them a cool down kit. Items in the kit may be things like drawing paper, pencils, a journal, play dough, a coloring book. Things your child finds relaxing. Make them a kit of these things and put it in spot where they can sit quietly to calm down.

We are all human. We make mistakes. We have feelings. God wired us that way. We all get angry sometimes. We just need to help kids learn to manage their feelings better and in a less harmful way.

Little People, Big Feelings

We all know at least one kid who seems extra sensitive. They cry over the smallest of things. What do we as adults do to help these kids who seem to cry and fall apart over things that seem so little or trivial? They have a hard time regulating their emotions. Their parents are worn out and frustrated because they feel like they have messed up as a parent, or they just cannot seem to figure out why this is happening all the time.

Children are always learning new things. Some things just take time to learn how to deal with. Emotions are one of those things. Some kids seem to cry or have meltdowns over the littlest things. They just fall apart at the mention of something outside of what they see as normal.

Things to be aware of when you have a sensitive child would be, have they eaten lately? Sometimes just being hungry can really mess with someone's mood. Is there something that is causing upset in another part of your child's life? Is there some kind of crisis or drama that is happening at school or home that can be causing your child to have meltdowns more than normal?

What can be done to help? Some parents and caregivers feel helpless. Little ones need to learn what feelings are and how to deal with them. This can really be a struggle and a true learning experience for children.

One of the biggest things I do when counseling children is help them identify their feelings and what to do when they have them. Kids feel those feelings they just do not know what they are or how to deal with them. There are many ways to go about this. I read them books on feelings, use games and flash cards, and many other resources to help the child learn about feelings and how they affect them.

The first step is to talk about feelings and help children identify when they are having feelings that do not feel so good what they can do about it. If your child appears to be upset by something then acknowledge their feeling. Something like, "I see that you are angry. Is there something I can help you with?" Help your child label the feeling, if you can in the moment. I know this is easier said than done, especially when you the parent are upset too.

Some kids you can tell that their anger is just building and they are going to blow. Think of a bottle of soda that has been all shook up! Try to catch them before reaching that point. I know this is hard at times and cannot always happen. I talk to kids all the time about feelings and help them say what they feel. This works well as long as their parent can listen to what they are feeling. If their parent or other adult, does not listen to how they feel then children will not tell their feelings.

For some kids, feelings can be very scary things, especially in cases that they are very sad, scared, or angry. These are very big feelings to deal with. A child's reaction is not always going to go well. They are going to have meltdowns and fall apart. This is part of learning to deal with feelings. You as the adult need to try to stay as calm as you can so that you do not add to the chaos. I know easier said than done.

Some kids let things bottle up so much that they keep things inside and they have other things happen like anxiety or depression. If kids are told for so long things like "oh, that isn't how you feel," or "your feeling is wrong." They stop telling people how they feel. It comes out in different ways. They find unhealthy ways to cope with feelings, anger outburst, meltdowns, and these then can turn into anxiety and depression. As well as bigger problems as they get older, substance use, suicidal thoughts, and rebellious behavior.

Keep in mind when working with children who seem extra emotional; is there a reason for their extra emotions? What are they going through? What is happening to them or in their family that could be upsetting them? Changes or transitions in life can really cause disruption to a child's routine. These could be little changes or big ones. But, keep in mind to little ones everything is a big deal. Adults need to be their safety net and help them learn to cope.

Some things that can be done to help cope is distraction. Help them find something else to do or redirect them if possible. Be available for your child to talk to. Listen to what they have to say. Sometimes just holding them and letting them cry is what they need. Have some items handy that help them calm down. Make them a calming kit. Things like a favorite stuffed animal, play dough, music, coloring books, puzzles, or other quiet activities.

If your child still is having issues with their emotions, or there is some big life issue that is affecting them please find them appropriate help. We as adult expect children to act like adults and be able to deal with life. Well, this is unrealistic! First, they are children! They are learning how to deal with emotions. Second, we have all seen adults that sometimes honestly act like children having a meltdown. Feelings are hard to keep in check even as adults.

Please, asking as a mental health professional who works with these children, allow your child to have their feelings. They need to have their feelings acknowledged. Their feelings are their feelings. When you do this they will know that you are listening to them and can help them. They feel safe with you. This is what we all want to happen. Help them talk through their feelings, even at the little age of three. Little people have feelings too!

The Feelings Doctor is In.

A few years ago, I had a young client came to see me for the first time. He wanted to know what my job was. I explained to him that I would be helping him with his feelings and talk about how to handle them better. He thought for a minute. Then he says, "So, you're a feelings doctor?" I laughed and then thought about his question. I said, "I guess I am." I now proudly accept that label.

We go to the doctor when we do not feel right physically. We may be sick, have a ongoing illness or disease that we need to seek regular care for, or we had some kind of physical health crisis like an injury. So, should not mental health be the same way? Should not we be able to seek professional help when we do not feel right mentally? Why is it such a stigma? Having a check up on your emotions and mental health is like having an annual physical. We should be able to seek professional help and not feel shamed by it.

What about a mental health crisis or emotional crisis like a death, trauma, or some other issue? Children, teens and adults all need a little help from time to time. Some are lucky to have a very good support system and they can handle most of what life throws at them. Sometimes things just hit us out of nowhere. Then there are people who seem like their lives are in constant chaos and have very little supports.

As a lifelong church attending Christian, I have seen other Christians tell people when they seek help say things like, "well, if you have more faith it will go away or be better."

What?!!! The amount of faith you have or do not have has nothing to do with it. Sometimes things in life just happen. Sometimes that person struggling with depression or anxiety have a chemical imbalance and they need medication to help them.

We as Christians need to understand that everyone needs Jesus, but someone may need a professional counselor to help them deal with their mental health just like someone with diabetes needs to have insulin to help them. God wired us to have emotions. He knows our feelings, and He has placed Christian Mental Health professionals in our lives to help us when we need it the most.

Just like you go to your physician for your physical health when you need it, some more than others, you may need to seek mental health services to help get your feelings checked. Please do not make excuses for why you do not want to go. If it is a matter of needing support, then find a supportive person to help you.

When I start working with one of my kid clients, we start with the basics of identifying feelings and when they feel that feeling. We play games, we read books, we talk about feelings. Do not be afraid to talk about your feelings with a safe person.

We adults need a safe person too. We need someone we can talk to and know that the conversation is kept to themselves. Adults need to have safe friends and supports too. We cannot do life alone. God has wired us to be in community with each other and help each other, and give support when needed.

When you are getting ready for your child to go back to school, do a mental health checkup too. As an adult if you just do not feel yourself. If you seem down or sad or worrying a lot, then it may be time to seek help for yourself. Yes, it may be hard to find help, but ask around. Talk to your supports, your pastor, a friend, your primary care doctor to see if they know of anyone who can help you. Your mental health is just as important as your physical health. Find yourself a good "Feelings Doctor" and start to feel back to yourself again soon.

I'm Wigging Out!! Anxiety and Kids

Anxiety for kids and teens is becoming more of an issue. I see kids with anxiety in counseling all the time. What is causing all the stress? Why is anxiety becoming such a problem? There are so many reasons why this is happening.

School is a big stressor for many kids. Kids stress about the amount of homework or school work they are expected to do. They have conflicts with peers that many times can be considered as bullying. There are more and higher expectations for kids in school now then ten or even fifteen years ago. Kids are under a lot of pressure to do well.

Kids get to the point they do not want to go to school anymore because of the stress and anxiety that it causes. They end up having meltdowns about homework and grades. I have talked to several of my client kiddos about this. I talk to them about not putting pressure on themselves with grades and school. I tell them to do their best they can do.

Kids also stress out about sports and other extra-curricular activities. These activities should be fun, not stressful. They should be a way to show school pride, have fun, and make friends, not cause stress and worry.

Kids also stress out about things at home. There may be issues at home like parents fighting, siblings, chores, homework, family activities, and so on which can cause some kids stress. Kids need down time just like anyone else. They need a routine. They need to let their little bodies rest. I know some families have a rule something like only one extra activity at a time or per marking period.

Signs to watch for in kids of anxiety would be complaints of stomach or headaches. Having a hard time settling down at night, or a hard time sleeping, because they are worried about getting things done, outbursts, meltdowns, crying fits, especially if these come out of nowhere or for no apparent reason.

Ways to help your anxious child could include reassuring them that everything will be okay. If they are being bullied help them figure out how to deal with the bully. If there are problems at home then reach out for help. Make yourself available to your kids so they can talk with you if needed. Create a calming home environment, so when they get home they can just relax. Set rules or boundaries when needed for how your child spends their time. Make priorities and stick to them.

Hopefully, this will help your child not "wig out" over things so easy. Stress and anxiety are hard on kids and their parents. Both sides at times feel helpless. If you feel stuck or helpless then reach out for help. Talk to the school, your pastor, the teacher, a counselor, or a trusted parent for direction.

Kids worry....at school

Do you have a child who does not want to go to school most of the time? Do they struggle with liking school? Do they have poor grades? Do they get bullied on a regular basis? Does your child struggle with making true friends? Do you as a parent make your child's education a priority?

Many kids struggle with anxiety when it comes to school. They do not feel safe at school for one reason or another. They are getting picked on or bullied by others. They feel like their teacher does not like them. A child's grades are low because they are having a hard time with understanding what it is, they are being taught.

They dread school because somewhere along the line they have had conflict of some kind, if it is with a teacher or a fellow student. Every child has had this happen at least once in their school career. The trick is helping a child or teen be able to push through the situation and move on.

How can this be done? Talk with your child or teen. Be available to listen when they have had a bad day, week or year. Be aware of who they are hanging out with and who they consider "friends." Take measures as parents to make home the safe place. School can be downright scary and cruel.

Make your home the safe place not only for your kids but, their friends too. Be aware of who may be upsetting your child and what you as a parent can do about it. Go to your child's school and help out. Watch the other kids in the school and the teachers. This helps your child to know that you are present and involved.

Make sure your child or teen's school work is done before any other activity like say video games or watching television. Children and teens need to understand that school work comes first. Sometimes this means making hard choices between school work and sports or other activities. If your child is struggling with subject or two get them help. Sit down with your child and see if you can help or someone else can. Yes, they will fight you on this and make it look like they are fine, but the proof is in the grades.

Now the flip side of this is, if your child is trying their absolute best, and they still are pulling "Cs" please understand that may be the best work your child can do. Some students are just not good at a particular subject. Be aware of your child's strengths and their weaknesses. Accept them for who they are and love them for the grade that they tried and worked for.

Kids have all kinds of reasons to not like school, but for the most part education and school should be enjoyable on some level. If they have friends that are good to them and are doing their best work and getting the best grades, they can then your child or teen should have their anxiety and stress level down to a healthy level.

Don't Use the "S" Word...(Stupid)

The "s" word drives me crazy! When we say someone is stupid that means you are talking about a person's intelligence. To me it is even worse using this word with kids. Because they believe whatever adults say. It becomes their inner voice. If you say a child is stupid then they believe you and this stunts their willingness to learn and grow.

I have seen this little word with big meaning shut a child down to learning or anything else for that matter. They believe they are stupid so why even try to learn. This word takes up space in their minds and sometimes just sets up camp. This word is hard to get out of a person's mind once it is there. This word damages a child's self-esteem. It damages how they view themselves as a person. This can very easily carry over to adulthood.

Kids have learning issues and they struggle all through school. Their peers see this and begin to use the dreaded "s" word. Kids call the kids who struggle stupid because they compare themselves to them. "Well, I got an "A" so that makes me a smarter student the Johnny." Then "Johnny" begins to believe his peers. They really struggle with school and it becomes not only a learning issue, but also an emotional issue. The kid who struggles gets easily frustrated and emotional. They just want to give up.

There are also adults who call kids around them the dreaded "s" word too. They joke about how smart or not smart their kid is. Parents, please stop this! It is not a joke! Kids begin to think your jokes are true. Then there are parents, very few, mind you, but they are there who call their kid stupid all the time. This is emotional abuse!! This must stop! You are doing emotional damage to your child. You are their parent. You need to be helping and encouraging your child, not tearing them down!

If they come home with school work you do not understand then you need to find someone who can help them. Sit and read with your child, help them with their homework. Show them school and learning are important.

I have had kids come to me in tears, and in defeat because someone they love, and who says loves them calls them stupid. This is heartbreaking. Then people like myself try to reprogram these kids to help them understand they are not stupid, far from it.

Remember we are all created in God's image. God does not make junk! If we are loving kids like Jesus, we need to encourage them to do well in everything they do. They can do it, they just need some extra help!

Chapter 2—Children's Ministry

Children's Ministry

I have been involved in several churches and in their children's ministries. I started out teaching in the children's program in the small church I grew up in. I also helped with things like Vacation Bible School and other children's programs. Most of the time I wrote my own lessons because there was very little for a budget to cover the cost of curriculum.

When I went to Bible College, I also had opportunities to serve in children's ministry. I would help at churches around me when I was able. I also went on mission trips to Georgia to lead a camping retreat for a home for pregnant teen girls. We would provide lessons and do day trips together with them.

My first for foreign mission trip was to Mexico. This was my senior year of Bible College. Part of my responsibilities included with providing activities and lessons for the kids in the church we worked in. My next four foreign mission trips were to the Dominican Republic. I loved these trips! They challenged and humbled me in so many ways.

The first time I went to the Dominican Republic, I talked to the national women from several churches about children's ministry. Talk about humbling and overwhelming! Not to mention teaching through an interpreter was interesting! The ladies of course were wonderful and the experience was definitely a good lesson for me.

Each time I went to the Dominican Republic my responsibility was to prepare activities for the children of the villages we were to visit. They referred to them as Vacation Bible School. We typically had about two or three hours and a flood of children!! Each time before our team left it was my responsibility as well as the others who helped with the kids programing to prepare lessons, music, crafts, gather supplies, and plan games.

I loved this! It was so much fun and such a challenge to put these Vacation Bible Schools together. There were times we had over 200 children attend. We also would visit a feeding center to help distribute meals to the children in the village. These children were so happy to see us and to play with us. It was very hard to leave them behind.

My first paid position in a church as an Inner-City Missionary. I raised support as a missionary would to be in this ministry. My focus was children's ministry. I had a great team of friends to work with. We definitely did ministry outside of the box. We had to. We had no budget. We relied on others to help us from within the church and outside of the church. It was an inner-city church in Lansing, Michigan.

We did things like Vacation Bible School for the neighbor kids. We would feed the kids breakfast every Sunday morning. We would do lessons and plan ways to reach out into the neighborhood we were ministering in.

My next paid ministry was working for Youth for Christ in the Teen Parent program. We would mentor teen parents and their young children. Part of my job was not only ministering to the teen parents, but also their young children. I created a curriculum to be used when the moms were in their meeting and their children were in a play group.

In each church I have been involved in, I have been part of the Children's Ministry. The church I currently attend is no exception. I teach Sunday School to second and third graders. This is my favorite age to teach! They are so fun! We have our lessons. We hang out and talk. We play games and do crafts. Any child who comes in my class knows they are loved! Since I do not have children of my own, I love on my Sunday School kids extra!

Part of loving kids like Jesus is correcting them when they need it. Part of being an effective Children's Ministry leader is being able to manage your classroom of students. This can be a challenge for even the most seasoned teacher or leader. We walk a fine line between making church fun but also keeping things in order so kids do not get hurt.

There is a variety of things I have learned over my years of teaching. Some of them the hard way! I set rules at the beginning of class so kids know and remember the expectations I have in class. Some of them are simple and what you would expect in any classroom setting. Things like raising your hand to be called on, being respectful to others, taking turns, and so on.

Some little tricks I have learned through the years from other teachers, I have become very helpful are things I have added to my tools in teaching kids. I have a talk object. What is a talk object? In my case I have a turtle beanie (for anyone who know me I collect turtles!). We named the turtle "Bubbles." Whoever has "Bubbles" is the person who gets to talk, including the teacher. This is a good visual for kids so they remember who's turn it is to talk.

Another thing I do, is at the beginning of each school year, when we promote kids to the next grade, and I get new kids I ask them what they like to do. The normal answers I get are things like crafts, coloring, and games. I them will rotate these things into my lessons. I try to find a coloring page for them to do or some kind of craft most weeks. Then every once in a while, I will do a game. I have games I have either purchased or have made. We play Bible Trivia, Sword Drills, or some other Bible learning game. This helps them have fun and reinforces what they have been learning in class. When we play games, I make sure there is some kind of prize or candy.

As a teacher, I am also not above bribery. At the end of class I give my kids a treat, usually a sucker. They know there are rules in order to get their sucker. This is also a fun way to send them out of class for the morning. It is just another way for me to show my kids that I love them like Jesus. I think that Jesus would give kids in His Sunday School class a treat. Just my opinion!

Kids and Missions

I have always encouraged my kids to be involved in missions. I have been involved in mission trips both state side and international. I have tried to find ways for kids to learn about missions. One of the things I do with my Sunday School class something we made up a few years ago that we call "Flat Paul."

I found a clip art of a Bible character and printed him off and laminated him. He became our "Flat Paul." "Flat Paul's" job is to travel to visit different missionaries in different countries. While he is there, he is to find out what the missionaries do and what the country is like and then to report back to our class about what he did.

My Sunday School kids love this, because they learn so much about helping others and to about other missions in other countries. We have a world map in our class where we mark with pins and string to show where the countries are where "Flat Paul" has visited.

A Little Girl with a Mission

One of my girls in Sunday School a few years ago, went on her first mission trip with our church and her family. She went to Haiti to visit a school our church supports. When she returned her and her friend who also went on the trip decided they wanted to collect dolls for the little girls in the school. She wanted to do this because she loved dolls so much that she wanted other girls in Haiti to have a doll too.

My little girl came to me with her idea to collect dolls. We talked to her parents and others in the church. By the next time she went on her next mission trip several months later we had collected over one hundred black dolls to take to her new friends in Haiti. Not only did we collect them, we cleaned them and a lady in the church who loves to sew made clothes for the dolls who needed them.

When adults say kids cannot do something because, they are kids are just wrong! They can if they have the backing of the adults around them. It was a fun project to do because at her age it was something she could be involved in and she felt of use to the little girls in Haiti.

This Little Light of Mine

This little light of mine, I'm gonna let it shine…. If you grew up in church you sang this song in Sunday School. We are called to let our lights shine so the world can see Jesus. If we are loving kids like Jesus, we are to let our lights shine to these little ones too. We let our lights shine so they know who they can come to when the need help. God calls us to be shining examples to the whole world, this includes the children God has put in our lives.

Have you ever been camping and had to use a flashlight because it was so dark? That is the only light you see in the darkness. Without it, you would not be able to see anything around you. The light may not be very bright, but it is there. Now imagine other campers join you with their flashlights. There is more and more light being added to your single light.

We let our lights shine no matter where we are, school, work, church, home, the grocery store, the world. Our light shines when we share the love of Jesus with those around us. For some we may be the only light they see in their dark world.

Kids today have so many things to deal with from a very young age in this dark world. To be a light for these kids gives them hope in a hopeless world. Our lights as adults need to shine bright for these hurting and struggling children.

The other thing we are called to do as adults, is to not only be a light, but to encourage and help children to be a light to their friends and peers. I have talked to my Sunday School kids many times about being a friend to someone who needs a friend, to help someone who is having a bad day, to be respectful to their teachers and other adults.

Kids need to learn to let their lights shine in a dark world too. I read stories of kids who do big things. They raise money for a cause they believe in, they help a kid who was really struggling, they reach out to help someone in need. They let their light shine in a dark world. If you are loving kids like Jesus then we should be teaching them to be lights too.

There is so much darkness and hurt in this world. We need as much light as we can get! In the gospel of Matthew chapter five, Jesus tells us to be salt and light in reaching out to a world that is dark and dying. Kids are dying every day be suicide. This needs to end. We need to be a light and teach the children we work with to care about others too. I tell my Sunday School kids they may not like someone but they need to at least respect them.

This little light of mine, I am gonna to let it shine…. Let your light shine in a dark and hurting world. Love kids like Jesus and shine your light for them.

Even Church Kids Need Help Sometimes….

Your family goes to church. You are involved in church. You teach your children all about God and how He loves them. That is great, but you and your children still live in the world. Your kids still have issues. They have hurts of this life that they just may not know how to deal with, and you as their parent do not know how to help them.

The problems of this world still affect you and your children. There is still divorce, abuse, bullies, death, and so on. Your child still needs someone they can talk to, a professional sometimes. Just because you or your child need counseling, does not make you a weak person or mean that you are not a good parent or a good Christian. It just means you need help.

How as a parent do you find a true Christian counselor for yourself, or your family? Just because it says "Christian" on the door may not make it true. Ask your pastor who they would recommend. I have pastors tell me time and time again they will not recommend someone unless they have met them and talked to them to know they are a Christian in word and deed. When you talk with a counselor that says they are a Christian ask them if they use scripture or biblical principles to counsel. You will get a good idea pretty quick whether they do or not.

When someone asks me questions about how I counsel and use scripture, my response is typically along the lines of, I use it all the time. If I know that you or your child is a Christian, and that is why you have sought me out, I tell them point blank that we will pull out the Bible and use it as we are talking. I will share with your child biblical concepts like "treat others the way you would like to be treated." Or I will use concepts from the Bible to talk about things like anger and sin. (I have taught Sunday School for many years!)

When you or your child needs help, reach out to your church family. Talk to your pastor or your youth pastor and see what they can do to help you. When your child is hurting pray with them and for them, I am sure you do this already! Let your child know that you are praying for them. Be available to them for when they need to talk. Talk to them about biblical concepts that can help them in their situation.

I have had many kids who come from good Christian homes, who struggle with things like depression, anger, anxiety, stress, bullies, school, peers, and so on. I have had teens tell me that they think about hurting themselves. These are teens that come from good Christian homes with good Christian parents. Satan is alive and at work! If he cannot take you out, he will go for your kids!

Kids need to learn how to handle the problems of life in a godly way. They need to understand who they can go to in time of need and hurt. They need to know who they can trust. This is a conversation parents need to have regularly with their children. You as parents need to talk to them about other adults that you trust and who can help your child, if you are not available or able.

I do not have kids of my own, but I make it very clear to my church kids and other kids I come in contact with that they can ALWAYS come to me. I make myself available to kids at church if they need to talk to me. I try very hard to be a person that not only do kids trust, but so do their parents.

Your family needs to be in a church with an active children and youth program with adults who love on your children on a weekly basis. If this is not happening, then your family may need to find a new church home. A church is not a building; it is the people who are inside of it that make it a family.

When your family is in trouble, or hurting there is no shame in seeking out help. Just because they live in a Christian home does not mean they will not try things like drugs or alcohol. It does not mean they will not feel sad or feel like they want to harm themselves. These are big issues parents, issues that most likely need the help of a professional, pray and seek out help! God may have just the right person there to help you or your child!

What to do with an angry kid?

You have figured out your kid has an anger problem, now what? There are many things that can be done to help your child. First, is figuring out what is triggering their anger. It could be many things. If they will not tell you, then you need to find a professional to help you. It could be something very serious. Most kids get angry over things like, divorce, death, school issues, friends, bullies, family issues, the bottom line is that until your child can talk about what is bothering them, there is not much that can be done to curb the anger.

They may not want to tell their parent for many reasons. They may fear getting in trouble. It may be that they are worried that their parent is already stressed, and they do not want to cause any more problems. They may be angry with their parent. They may be afraid due to an abuse or domestic violence situation.

Whatever the reason, if your child is not willing to tell you as their parent, then seeking professional help is what is needed. In most cases, it is easier for a child to tell a third-party person like a counselor than to talk to their own parent. If your therapist is a helpful one, they will include you as the parent in the counseling so the anger issue can be resolved.

The other thing that your friendly, helpful counselor can do is give your child ways of coping with their anger. There is a reason for the anger, with the help of the counselor, it can be figured out. Also, the counselor can help your child with coping strategies to help defuse their anger when it hits. Things like taking a break or time out, or learning breathing techniques, or being able to label feelings can all be very helpful, and things like your child being able to say that they are angry or sad. Sometimes, kids have a hard time being able to identify their feelings for what they are.

Having ways of distraction, when they are upset about something major like death or divorce can also help. It can help your child direct their frustrations to something productive, or they can talk about what is really hurting them. These children are hurting and they need to be able to voice their hurts. If they are not able to then. it just gets buried, and becomes a bigger problem. This is how things like drug and alcohol use or anxiety start.

Parents need to remember children are learning how to control their emotions. Kids are going to have meltdowns., it is a normal developmental stage. Especially, in the early years for toddlers and preschoolers, and other stages as well, like middle school years. It is our job to give kids ways to learn self-control, things like walking away or telling a trusted adult when someone has hurt them is very important.

We can help them make all kinds of little crafty things to help them redirect their focus and be a visual reminder. Pick one or two of these things and use them well. Make sure what you pick is something your child can do themselves and use to actually help them. We do not want to give them a stress ball to squeeze when they are upset, if all they are going to do is throw it at someone!

Helping your child figure out what triggers their anger is also important. What or who is upsetting your child? Is it a teacher, a peer at school, a situation, or even you their parent? Figuring this out is so important, in helping getting a handle on your child's anger. We can give them all these tools to help with anger, which will help some, but until figuring out what is triggering your child it is just going to keep going in a cycle.

Your child's anger and other feelings need to be validated. Your child needs to feel heard. This will help break down walls of communication. If your child knows that you listen, then they are more willing to tell you what is upsetting them. You may not as a parent, be able to fix it for them, but you can find someone who can help. A child being angry all the time is not a healthy thing for anyone. It causes stress not only for your child, but everyone around them, including you the parent. They do not like feeling angry anymore then you like to see them angry. Do not be afraid to reach out to get help for your angry child. They will thank you for it later!

Can I Ever Do Anything Right?

Can I ever do anything right? Children ask this question to themselves so many times in their life time. Some more than others. Kids who constantly have behavior problems, feel like they are always in trouble. They are always being corrected for their behavior, sometimes this is very needed. Some children need more reminders then others. They feel like they are always being watched. What do they hear when they FINALLY do something right? Do they hear praises for their right choices? Some do not.

I have worked with many difficult children and teens, in my career of working with children in a variety of ways. Kids that are the hardest to love, are often the ones who need it most. They need to know that they do something well or right! What happens if this does not happen for them? They begin to care less and less about life. They struggle with things like anxiety, depression, anger, resentment, and so on.

Every kid needs to hear things like, "nice job," "you are awesome," or even "I love you!" Many kids do not hear these positive statements. When kids do something that they are changing for the better they need to hear feedback that they are doing good! If they do not hear these things, they will not want to keep that change in their lives because they will not see a point.

Sometimes these kids who struggle. they often feel like they cannot do anything right. They often feel like they have a target on their back, or they have been labeled the "bad kid." This may come from school, friends, teachers, or other adults. To these kids they are honestly trying, they know that what they do is wrong. They just struggle when making the right choice. Some days are better than others.

How do we handle these kids who really struggle with making good choices? We help them work through why their choice was wrong and how to fix it. Helping them learn from their mistakes and move on.

We as adults seem to think that kids are expected to know how to behave all the time. and kids should just know how to behave. This is so far from the truth. They are kids! Then add things like trauma and learning issues that makes it harder. Kids learn to behave by having consistent rules and expectations. Some children do not have this in their home, this adds another part into their behavior.

As a caregiver, you need to be the adult and meet this child where they are, not where YOU want them to be. As an adult there may be things that you let slide as long as they do not hurt themselves or others. Sometimes, it is a matter of picking your battles. Keep this in mind when correcting these kiddos that just do not seem to get it sometimes!

The bottom line, is kids want to be loved and cared for. Some kids need this more than others. Help kids feel better about themselves by speaking positive things in their lives. Remember for every negative thing a child hears they need to hear three positives to cancel it out. Just imagine how it feels to hear nothing but negative. Put yourself in that child's shoes. How would you feel if all you heard was negative? Now take that thought and go be a positive influence in a negative world.

Love Me When I Am Naughty

Kids make mistakes, we all do. Kids are learning right from wrong. It is our job as adults to teach them right from wrong. It is also our job to discipline them when they do something naughty. If we love kids like Jesus this comes with the job. Jesus wants us to act more like Him. That takes discipline and correction when we make mistakes, kids included.

We are called to love the sinner, but hate the sin. Many years ago, I worked with pregnant and parenting teens. I was asked by a fellow Christian who I looked up to, how could I work with girls who did these things? I responded with, we all sin, theirs is just more obvious than some of the rest of us.

We live in a broken world. Sin happens, we need to learn how to love kids through their sin. Kids make some pretty big mistakes. Some cause great consequences. Just because kids make a mistake does not mean they do not deserve to be loved.

Many times, kids do naughty things to get attention. They feel like they do not get the attention they need so they are willing to get it any way they can. They do not care if it is positive or negative attention. To them, attention is attention.

Some kids are testing their limits with you by doing something naughty. They want to see if you will do what you say you will do or not. If you make a threat to discipline, then you need to follow through with it. One of my boys would act up in class. I would tell him, "I have Grandpa on speed dial." He knew when I said that to him, he needed to straighten up or I would call his Grandpa. Yes, a few times I had to call Grandpa.

Part of loving kids like Jesus, is also giving grace to a kid who is having a hard day. Maybe they had a rough morning. Maybe there are problems at home. Maybe they do not feel well or they are tired. A reminder may be enough for them. They may need a listening ear. Maybe they got into an argument with a sibling. Adults have bad days and so do kids.

Kids who have a rough home life tend to act out because they are crying out for help. Maybe they are afraid to go home because of what happens there, so they do things so they can stay at school or where ever they feel safe. For example, they may act up at school because they get detention after school so they do not have to go home right away.

Loving kids like Jesus means setting limits. There are rules for a reason. Kids like to test those limits. Some kids REALLY like to test those limits. It is good to set boundaries with children so they know what they can and cannot do with you. Kids want to know where they stand with you.

Some kids act out and do naughty things because they try to see if you will reject them. If they keep you at a distance that is keeping them safe. They most likely have been hurt by adults in the past, and so therefore they act out to see if you stay away from them. It is our job in loving them like Jesus to love them extra and push through this, because once you do that child has something they have never had before, unconditional love!

Loving kids like Jesus is a tough job. It takes lots of work! Kids are crazy! They do some crazy things that we just want to shake our heads at. I have had my share of challenging kids in my career of working with children. I have kids who were so tough in my Sunday

School class who are now teens and young adults who are just amazing to watch! They have come through their hard times to be responsible young adults.

The kids who need the most love will ask for it in the most unloving of ways. This is why we are called to love them like Jesus, so they can feel unconditional love, sometimes for the first time in their young lives!

Being the Hands and Feet of Jesus

Working with children can be a very dirty job in more ways than one. There are days I come home with play dough stuck to my fingers and marker on my hands. It can also be emotionally dirty or draining too. There may be kids or families that working with them or talking to them drains you. Their situation is rough. You want to protect these children from further harm.

I have to put myself in check, I cannot take home every hurting kid. It is not good to bring my work home with me. What do I do instead? I do everything within my power to help the child or family in my care. If I have to, I call and report abusive situations. I reassure the child that part of my job is to make sure they are safe. If I need to, I help with things like food, clothes, and school supplies. I have resource lists and connections to help with these things.

Loving kids like Jesus is not easy. It is not all fun and games all the time. Yes, playing them for sure is the fun part! God calls us to more. He calls us to teach, to correct, to love and to help these little ones in our lives. Kids need to know that you love them enough to tell them when they are doing something unkind or harmful. They look to adults for protection and direction.

Part of being the hands and feet of Jesus is to do something with a child. Mentor them, hang out with them, talk to them on their level, interact with them! How do you help a child? First, is to be on their level, sometimes literally! Get on the floor and play with them. Play a game they like or just sit and color with them. When I talk with kids I many times get more information from them by just playing with them than anything else. I get out a game or play dough and we just talk and play. Most of the time this helps them have a more relaxing conversation with me.

Another part of being the hands and feet of Jesus, for a child is doing something on their behalf. Be their voice or advocate. Speak up for them, when they are too scared or worried to do it for themselves. Then also teach them to speak up for themselves. There are times I have to go to court to testify for them on their behalf. This is part of my job that I really do not like, but, I do it. I do it because it is necessary for adults to hear from me what the child cannot say for themselves.

If we are called to love kids like Jesus, we need to be the hands and feet of Jesus. We need to show the love of Christ by doing not just saying. Our actions speak louder than our words. Yes, working with kids and helping kids gets messy, but it can also be so much fun, and the rewards are amazing!

What Would Jesus Do?

Several years ago, a fad went through the Christian community asking the question "What Would Jesus Do?" It spread quickly with bracelets, t-shirts, and other wearable items. The idea of the question, was a daily reminder of what would Jesus do in the situations you come across daily. It was supposed to be a check in with yourself to remind you to act more like Jesus would.

Many people of all ages took it seriously. They would wear their bracelet every day to remind themselves how they should be treating others. The same idea applies to loving kids like Jesus. We are called to love those around us like Jesus would. We need make ourselves approachable to kids and youth. They know you are a person they can trust and come to. They can tell you the fun stuff and the scary or hard stuff too. They know no matter what, they can trust you.

When kids are sick or hurt, do you take time from your day to talk to them? To care for them? Kids have tragic things happen in their lives too. Research tells us that a child can survive something traumatic in their lives when they have adults and caregivers who support them and care for them during the hard and scary times of life.

I have had clients who have had parents die. Could you imagine being a little kid and losing someone like a parent? The adults around you are just as upset as you are. How do you function? Having trusted adults to help you to care for you is a big part of this. When I have had clients, who have had a parent pass away I have gotten them a comfort kit. Things that bring comfort for that child. Things like a stuffed animal, a journal, coloring books, crayons, play dough, maybe even a favorite treat. I then bring the kit to the child and talk with them. Just them. Make sure they know that I am there for them.

We teach the Golden Rule, "do unto others what you would have them do unto you." This is WWJD. How do we want to be treated? It would be a comfort for you if someone came to see you at a low point in your life and helped you? What about treating you with respect even when you may not be the most popular person?

Do we get treated the same? I would hope so, but if not, it will still be okay. Is that why we do nice things, so people will do nice things for us? If we treat others the way Jesus would want us to, just imagine what our world would be like!

We adults need to teach our children and youth to think WWJD. We need to teach them to treat others with respect and kindness, not for material reward, but for knowing it is the right thing to do. One of the basic things we teach kids from an early age is to share. Just image what our world would look like if we would help each other up instead of pushing each other down.

To love kids like Jesus many times means putting aside our own selfish needs and desires and asking "What would Jesus do?" Would He take time out to talk to a hurting child? Absolutely! Would He take time to listen to a lonely child? Yes! Jesus is calling us to do the same.

Are you going to answer the call? Are you going to WWJD? Are you going to love these kids like Jesus? Please do! If you do not, that child may not have anyone to show them the love of Jesus.

Chapter 3—Ministering to Children No Matter Where

47

All Kids need a Bubble –Boundaries for Children

We all know a child or two that wants to hug and touch everyone! At some point it crosses a line or two, others get frustrated. Like anything else with children, they need to learn boundaries. They need to know what they can and cannot do to adults and to other peers. For some children the concept of boundaries can be a very difficult thing for them to understand. It is something to be learned over a life time.

When I explain the concept of "boundaries" to children I usually try to use a visual illustration. I usually explain that having boundaries is like having a fence around you. Some things can go in and out, but not everything, and there is a gate to allow the safe people in and out as you choose. I also use the visual of having a personal bubble. This helps children understand that everyone has their own space and when we cross that bubble or someone crosses their bubble it can make someone feel uncomfortable.

Why is teaching children "boundaries" so important? This not only protects them, but also protects others. Children need to understand that everyone has limits and that those limits need to be respected, including their own. This helps the child to understand they do have control over who they interact with and to what extent. If they do not want to hug someone, do not force it. Your child may not be in the mood for a hug or, they may not trust that person. Myself personally, I ask the children I interact with if they would like a hug. I leave it up to them. If they say "no" then I just let it be. I may offer a high five or fist bump instead.

This teaches your child that it is okay to tell others "no" when they do not want to do something. This includes playing with other children. Your child may not want to play with another child because they may not be in the mood to play with them, or the other child has been rude or mean to them. Let them choose who they play with, and then of course as long as the other child is a good influence.

We also need to teach children that others have boundaries. Some children really struggle with keeping their hands to themselves. They want to touch and grab someone or something all the time. I know this can be frustrating to all involved. Some children also struggle with boundaries when they are angry. They may lash out and hit another child, this needs to of course be addressed and taken care of, but, all of these things are "boundary issues."

For some children who struggle with Asperger's Syndrome they struggle with social interaction in general. They also struggle with reading social ques like facial expressions and body language.

For these children, teaching boundaries may be more in depth. They need to learn to identify feelings and what it may look like when someone is angry or frustrated.

The same goes for children who have experienced some sort of abuse. They are either very fearful of others and shy away, or they are looking for whatever attention they can get, so therefore they hug and touch whoever they like or see. These things of course can cause many problems.

The concept of "boundaries" needs to be taught from an early age. Children need to learn what is okay to do and what is not okay. As parents and caregivers, we have a responsibility to teach these things to the children entrusted to our care. For some children it is easier than others. Like anything it takes patience and practice when working with children on this issue.

Be a Shining Star in a Dark World

As you and your children gear up to go back to school, remember something, to be a support for not only your child but your child's friends. Your child's friends may not have the best home life. They may be living in a single parent home where their parent may work extra hours to make ends meet. Many children live in a home where both parents work so they may have limited time with their parents. There may be stress or issues in the home where children do not want to be at home because of the tension this creates.

Where do we find these kids? They may be your child's friends, your family member, a classmate, a neighbor. They are all around you. I know you have your own kids to worry about getting to practice and getting homework done, but what if you became that home where children felt safe and loved. What if your home turned into a place where your child's friends felt like they could come hang out, eat a snack, do their homework, and they felt like someone cared? What impact do you think that would have?

The single mom would know their child was some place where they were safe and cared for, so she would not be worrying about them while she worked. The working family who are just struggling to get by would know their child is being looked after by a trusted adult.

The child who comes to hang out in your home would feel safe. They would learn to trust other adults even when other adults have let them down many times before. They would have an example of what a "normal" family looked like. They would have friends they could hang out with and play with who were a good influence. They would have an adult who would listen to them when they have had a bad day. They would feel heard.

I know this is a mighty task as a parent. It does not need to be every day and it does not need to be all evening. I know caring for other children can be stressful and not easy. Maybe you are a single parent too. Maybe you work something out with another single parent where you trade days so you can help each other out.

Be a light to the children, teens, and families around you. See what you can do as a parent, a stay at home mom or dad, an aunt or uncle, to make a positive difference in the life of not only a child but their family as well. Be that light shines in a dark world. There are so many negative things happening that would not it be amazing if as a community could help be stars shining bright in a world of darkness.

Fostering Hope

Jesus calls us to care for the orphans. He calls us to take care of the fatherless. In our country we have kids every day entering the foster care system. For many of them, for reasons that are so scary to even imagine. All these kids want is for someone to love them. If we are loving kids like Jesus this is a group of children we need to focus on.

Kids who are in foster care come from broken homes where they have had their hearts broken, not once, but too many times to even count. They need the love of Jesus. Who better to show them the love of Jesus then us? Now, loving these kids is not an easy job. They have been removed from their parents for some very scary reasons.

I know several people who have taken in foster kids and in some cases been able to adopt them. These families are a light in a storm for many children. For the first time, for many children, they have a stable home with parents who care for them. For many of these children, this is scary because they worry if they will be hurt or rejected.

Foster children come with so much baggage, because of the pain they have been through in their short lives. This baggage may be very hard to unpack and take a long time to do so. This is where love and patience and understanding all come into play. The simplest thing could trigger fear and anxiety for these children.

Many families take in these foster children in hopes of providing them a permanent home. The parents who open their homes to these children are showing love to children who may not have ever had love in their lives, ever!

Loving kids like Jesus can be a battle. We need to prepare ourselves. For many foster families they have a battle to fight with so many different groups and people. There is the court system, Child Protective Services (CPS), the bio family, the school, doctors, therapists, and so many more. These are battles that may not be easy but if all goes well are so worth it.

In the lives of these children, loving kids like Jesus means they end up in a home where they are loved and cared for, maybe for the first time. How can we help these children, even if we are not able to take in foster children?

We can help and support the families who do. We can advocate for these children as professionals. We can be a listening ear to not only the children, but also for the families who open their homes to them. It takes a village to raise a child, any child.

It Takes a Village

We have all heard the phrase, "It takes a Village." This is very true on many different levels. As a parent you cannot do everything yourself, and you cannot be all things to all people. Children and teens need a wide variety of helpers to get through life. They need to know there are others who can help them in a time when maybe, for some reason their mom or dad cannot.

As a parent, you want to protect your child from harm and hurt. Part of that is helping your child or teen, learn who they can trust in life. One thing I work on with children and teens to help them figure out who their support network is and who they can trust as we figure out who they can go to for help in many different places. For example, if they are at school, or church, or with other supportive adults they can seek out when they need something.

As parents, it is okay to reach out for help and teach your children to do the same. Helping your child find those safe people is part of developing healthy relationships with others. In helping you as a parent, help your child identify those "safe people." Start talking about who is a safe person and why. What makes them a safe person?

In the process of working with my clients, as a child therapist I start asking my clients to identify who in their lives help them? Most of the time, I get things like; mom, dad, aunts, uncles, siblings, grandparents, family friends, teachers, community members, and so on. Most of the time, my clients can tell me who helps them and protects them, they know who is there for them and when. It is a matter of helping them break down why they trust that person or go to that person for help.

Then there is in some cases where a person who they once trusted is no longer there for whatever reason, or a trusted person has done something to lose trust in the eyes of the child. For example, leaving or abandoning them or hurting them in some way. This is part of the reason I help children find more than one or two adults. It takes a village.

As a trusted adult, what are you doing to help other children and teens who need someone they can trust? You may be a stay at home mom (or dad) whose child has a friend who needs a place to hang out after school for a couple of hours. Why not your house? You could be helping out a single parent, who may need an extra set of eyes, ears, or hands from time to time.

You may be a teacher who makes it very clear to their students that you can be trusted and will help your students in any way you can. You may be a mentor or coach who has a child on your team who does not have a dad. Do you have time to take that child fishing or to play at the park, or take them to dinner? You may have a neighbor who has lots of little ones and it struggling at Christmas. What can you do to help?

Look around for ways to serve and help others. If everyone gave a little time, money, and help our world would be a much better place! Living in a small town and watching how people invest in each other and help each other is such a blessing to watch and be a part of. You do not have to have lots of money to make an impact in a child's life. Every boy needs an uncle and every girl needs an aunt. Join the village to make an impact.

Run to the Safe People

As a child therapist I hear all the time that kids are scared to go to school. Usually it is because they are being bullied or picked on. They do not want to go to school because the bullies are being mean. Why should one child have that much control over another child? I was bullied in school as a child. I learned to stand up for myself, so the bullies would leave me alone! Sometimes is worked sometimes it did not.

Now I kids are afraid to go to school for another reason. They are afraid someone is going to hurt them or shoot them! The schools do lockdown drills, so kids know what to do if there is an "active shooter" in the building. WHAT!!!! How has our world come to this that people think this is okay? People are so angry with the world they would want to kill another person and children.

We can blame whoever we want, video games, bad parenting, violence on television, politicians or whoever else we can! The person who's fault this is, is the person with the gun! They are the bad guy!!! Do you remember when the "good guys" would take out the "bad guys" and protect the innocent? This needs to be put back into place! Kids and teachers need to feel safe going to school again!

We in American, have the right to have guns for protection. Many generations of military fought for this right! We have the right to protect the innocent from the "bad guys." If there is an active shooter then the people who have taken the proper steps to be able to carry a gun should be able to use it! That is why they have it, for protection!

I talk to many home-schooling families and one reason they give for home schooling their children is to protect them. Do you blame them? Seriously! Kids need to feel safe at school and right now many children do not feel safe!

Instead of teaching children to run away from the police, teach them to go to the police for help! That is why the police are there, to help! Police officers are painted as the "bad guys." Now, yes there are some police officers that do not do their job right, but does this mean we put them all in this category? NO!

Police officers put their lives on the line every day to help keep us safe, and what do they get in return? They get yelled at, cursed at, assaulted, blamed, and trash talked! All for little pay and they take time away from their families to do all of this! AND, their families worry whether their loved one will come home in one piece or not!

When I talk to children about "safe people" we talk about police officers. I want children to understand that police officers are there to keep them safe from the "bad guys." My dad was a police officer when I was a kid. He was a good police officer! All my friends knew he was a safe person. He would come to my school and talk to my classmates, so they knew he cared about them! He would hand out candy when he worked on Halloween to kids, so they knew police officers cared about them!

We need to go back to where the "good guys" can protect the innocent from the "bad guys." We need to go back to a time when the "bad guys" got in trouble for their actions and not just dismissed with an attitude of "don't do that again!" Let the "good guys" do their job so our kids can feel safe at school again!!

Being the Cool Teacher

Do you want to be the fun teacher? The one that kids run up and hug every time they see you? The answer is simple, care! That is right, care about those kids. Know what is happening in their lives. Ask them questions. Get to know them individually. Let down your guard of being an adult and get on their level, in some cases literally.

I have taught Sunday School for years. Every week I go around the room and ask the kids how their week was. If they had a good week or not so good week. You find out all kinds of things this way. I find out if they have a sick or hurt loved one, or if they themselves have been sick or got hurt. I find out things that are bothering them. It may be a little thing, but to them it is big. If they trust me with the little stuff, when they have something big, they will come to me.

Several years ago, I had one boy in my class who lives with his grandparents. His grandma is in a wheel chair and they boy then tells me that grandpa had broken his leg that week and just got out of the hospital. Did I mention there were five kids in the house?! We get through prayer time and I sprang into action! I went to some of the other ladies in the church and we organized a meal train to help them. We also set up rides so the kids could get to still do their normal activities. Whew! We would not have known had we not asked!

I had another boy who was being bullied on the school bus. He asked for prayers when riding the bus, he had tears in his eyes. I had him wait until after class so we could talk. He told me an older boy had threatened to shoot him on the bus with a gun. Well, no wonder he was scared. I talked to his mom and of course his parents handled the situation.

Part of being the "cool" teacher is doing fun things. What is more fun than a party? During holidays I plan parties for my kids. The Christmas parties are big for my kids. I of course get them a gift and we have treats, games and crafts. I want them to know they are loved and we can have fun at church too. I also do parties for Valentine's day and Easter. We do game days in class too. I bring some kind of game and of course prizes.

Being the "cool" teacher is not always easy. Kids still need to respect you, but you can do it in a way that is kind and loving. "My kids" know that I do not tolerate disrespect in class to anyone, not just me, but they also know that I love them. How do they know this? For one I tell them. Yes, I tell my church kids, I love them. I also show them I love them by how I treat them and take time to be there for them. Remember you may be the only Jesus they see.

Back to School, Back to Reality!

School starts every year just by the turn of the calendar. School supplies are being purchased. Classrooms are being set up. Teachers are preparing for a new year with new students. Students are picking out clothes and backpacks. Parents are grateful school will start soon. Students, not so much! They have enjoyed sleeping in, playing all day, and just doing nothing. Are your kids ready?

For some students, school is not so much fun for many different reasons. Some kids really dread school. There are many reasons, bullies, learning issues, lack of friends, "mean" teachers, homework and school work that frustrates them. These students may need a different kind of preparing. They find school stressful for many reasons. Of course, we all know about the issue of bullies. How can parents, teachers, and other caregivers help these students?

We can help by for starters, by listening to them. Listen when they have a good day or a not so good day. Help them see the positives in their day. Many times, we focus on the negatives in the day and not on the good stuff that happens. What did you have for lunch? What did you do at recess? Your friend was nice and helped you out today, great!

Also, help be an advocate for your student. Help them by giving a voice to the things that are bothering them, either, teach them to be their own voice or step in and help when they need it. Kids need to know they have grown up friends and helpers, who are willing to step in when they need help. Maybe just listening when they have had a rough day or helping with homework that is really hard for them.

For older students and teens, do not be afraid to monitor their social media and cell phones. Now, do this with them standing there with you. Go through their texts and social media to see who they are talking to. Help them to understand that, one you are watching and aware, and two you are watching out for others who may want to do your teen harm. Yes, they will argue with you and say that you are invading their privacy. You are being their parent! Yes, they need privacy, but they also need to know they are being held accountable. This will hopefully, weed out the trouble making kids in your child's life.

Talk openly with your child about their friends and what they do with them in school and outside of school. This shows that not only do you care about them but their friends too. Talk to your kids about their struggles and why they struggle. Your child may be a straight "A" student, but they really struggle with making friends. They may be totally flunking out of school, and struggling with how they feel about themselves.

Be aware of your child's friends and when they may come to you for help, because their parent is not available. They have identified you as a safe person, be their advocate too. Be their voice. If you see them struggling talk to them. Invite your child's friends to your home to hang out. If they need help with their homework, help them. Maybe, they live in a single parent home and their parent works and struggles with helping to get homework finished. Make your home that safe home. Let them come hang out after school until their parent gets home.

Be aware of what is going on around you as a parent or caregiver. If you see a child in need of extra help, then be their helper. Share extra school supplies, snacks, and time. I know it seems like a lot sometimes, but in the end, it means so much more to a kid who really needs to be heard!

Chapter 4—Meeting Them Where They Are

Bow Your Head Close Your Eyes....

One of our jobs as people who work with and love children like Jesus is to teach them to talk directly to God. It is our job to help them to pray and how to pray. Kids need to know that we cannot always be with them but God can! They can pray to God and talk to Him about anything! Kids pray for all kinds of things. This helps them build their faith in God. Kids also do not tend to worry about what to ask for from God. They come with childlike faith.

Just as it is import to teach kids to pray to God, it is also import that we as the adults who love them like Jesus is to pray FOR them! What do we pray for? Well, school, home life, friends, struggles, and even a sick cat or dog! If it is important to them, we pray about it. Now, do we pray for new toys, no! This is part of what we need to teach kids is to pray for what is important.

I close my Sunday School class with prayer. I ask what the kids need prayer for. I find out so much during this time. What they worry about, who is in their lives, what is happening around them. My church kids know I pray for them.

A few years ago, I had a few kids who were being bullied in school. Every Sunday we would pray for "the bullies to not be bullies." Wow! Talk about praying for your enemies! I wish adults could do this better. This group of kids taught me a good lesson about prayer. Instead of being angry at their enemies they prayed for them.

Hurting Kids Hurt People

Many people ask me as a counselor, how do I help my hurting kid? Parents and caregivers can see their child is hurting. This a problem that is not always easy to solve. You see, it is because some hurts are so big. It is not like a scrapped knee that gets a band aid and a kiss. I wish it was that simple. Believe me as I see kids sit across from me in tears because they cannot figure out why their parent does not come home or why someone who loves them so much would purposely hurt them.

Children naturally think anything that happens is because of something they did. For example, if mom and dad split up kids think if they would have behaved better or gotten better grades their parents would not have split up. When in reality, the parents split up for very adult reasons. This is how I explain it to my client kids so they hopefully understand that mom and dad getting a divorce, is not because of something they did.

When kids are hurting, there are some very basic things parents and caregivers can do to help. One, listen. Just be available for your kids to talk and do not judge what they are saying. Two, provide consistency. Do not let kids do naughty things and let them get away with it because, "they are having a hard time." Three, allow your child to be angry or sad. God wired us to have those feelings.

It is okay to have them and express them. I tell the kids I work with it is okay to be angry, but to not do naughty things in their anger. Lastly, find our child a qualified mental health professional who specializes in working with children to help. Look for a child therapist who knows and understands children and trauma.

When working with kids who are hurting, things can come up like depression, anxiety, stress, anger, acting out, as well as others. One way to support your child at home. is to offer a "safe space." This may be their room or some other place where they can get a way and just chill out.

Also, provide some kind of "cool down kits." Things in these kits could be activities that are quiet and calming to your child. Some sound cancelling headphones, coloring book and crayons, puzzles, books, music, or a journal just to list a few.

In cases where children or teens have made comments that they do not want to be around, or want to hurt themselves, PLEASE get help! This is not a game! Even if you think your child would not do anything, do you want to be wrong? Also, make sure to lock up all meds and sharp objects to keep them safe. Make a safety plan with them and their therapist. Do not be afraid to reach out for help so your child or teen can hopefully get the proper help they need, and deserve.

Don't Let Your Kid Have an Ugly Heart

Let's face it kids say what they are thinking. They do not have a filter. This is a teaching opportunity for adults to teach them what is appropriate and what is not appropriate to say. Kids say things out of curiosity, not knowing any different.

Then there are kids who are just flat up mean! They have an ugly heart. They say what they want, to whoever they want without any regard to people's feelings. They have not learned to be careful with what they say. They say hurtful words and do hurtful things because they have learned this behavior is okay to do. They have learned there are not consequences to their actions. The problem with this behavior is, who they leave in their wake of hurtful words in actions, their victims.

If we are loving kids like Jesus, we need to help both kids. We need to help the bully who is doing and saying the hurtful things, and we need to help the victim. Jesus tells us to turn the other cheek. How do we help the kids who are left hurt, and broken by the bullies? How many times are they supposed to "turn the other cheek?"

These are hard questions to answer, especially when your child is the victim. As a parent you want to protect your child from harm. You want to keep them safe from hurt and pain. The problem with this is we live in a broken and sin filled world. Jesus wants us to love our enemies and forgive those who hurt us. What? That kid over there just hurt my kid so bad they are crying, and do not want to go to school.

It is our job to help children love others like Jesus. Sure, it is easy to love our friends and people we like. It is not so easy to love the people who hurt us. One thing I share with kids I work with is, that some people are just mean. They think their behavior is okay. There is not much you can do, except pray for them and limit the time you are around them. We may not like everyone, but it is our job to respect them. They may not respect us, but we need to show them respect. It is between them and God how they treat others.

That however, does not mean to let them walk all over you. As a kid it is okay to get help. If someone is hurting your child they need to tell. Many schools have a "no bullying policy." The adults around your child cannot do anything to help them, if they are not aware of it. Many parents feel that it is okay for their child to stand up for themselves. I believe this is okay to a degree. It is okay to stand up for yourself, and defend yourself in a fight. Kids need to make sure there is no other way out. It is not okay to call names back and swing the first punch.

There are many steps that need to happen before fists start to fly. These steps need to be taught to kids. This is part of helping both sides of the argument or fight. We need to teach kids to use their words to solve their problems, not their fists. It is okay to tell a person who is calling you names or treating you poorly, to stop.

When a child is bullied it affects their self-esteem, their self-worth, peer interactions and so much more. I have seen so many kids in my counseling career who have been bullied. They have a hard time making friends. They question their abilities in so many areas of their lives. They have anger issues because, they see any peer as someone who could or may say something mean to them. Their guard is up all the time!

I was bullied as a child. I have scars on my body from having heart surgery when I was a baby. Kids would make fun of my scars and pick on me because of it. I was very self-aware of those scars. I know other kids who have scars on their bodies, who have had similar experiences of being called ugly, or something else because in some way they are different.

It took me a long time to realize my scars are not what defines me. I have created in the image of God, and without those scars I would not be here today.

Please do not let your child have an ugly heart. Teach them to see people for who they are on the inside, not their scars, whether physical or otherwise. We all have battle wounds of some kind; some are just easier to see.

EGR Kids (Extra Grace Required)

The saying, the kids who need love the most, ask for it in the most unloving of ways. Oh, how true this is! They are the most difficult kids in your class, your home, or in your office. They just drain you every time you are around them. They do some really crazy things! I do not mean the cute stuff either. They are a walking meltdown!

They may be the class bully, or the kid who just cannot seem to get a grip, or keep themselves together no matter how hard they try. They may have ADD or ADHD, or some other set of letters. They have this issue, but the issue should not define who they are. They should not be the "ADHD kid." They should not have this label attached to them as a way of telling who they are.

When interacting with these EGR kids, there needs to be grace and love. Excepting them for where they are, and not where YOU think they should be. For some people, including children, life is just harder. It is not something they have done necessarily.

The first thing we need to do, is love them no matter what. We may not like their behavior, but Jesus has called us to love them, no matter what. The other things we need to do for them is to set boundaries, or limits for them. This will help you and them. Try to do this in a kind and loving way. All kids need to know their limits. Most likely these EGR kids have not been taught limits or boundaries, or if they have it come in the form of abuse or inconsistently.

With EGR kids, it is best to try to not raise your voice. This is what they are used to. They are used to adults yelling at them, so they expect it. They think it is normal. They want to see how far they can push you and your limits.

Remember, God has put this child in your path for a reason. Maybe that reason is for them to experience having a loving, caring adult in their life for maybe, the first time ever. Most of the time kids do what they do for survival. For example, they may do things that are really silly, mean, or rude to see if they push you away first. If they push you away, then that means you are one less adult who will reject or hurt them. Do your best to push beyond this point.

If you want to change a child's behavior, then reward them in some way for the good behavior. Do some kind of "caught you being good" system. Many schools do this. The child earns points or something, else to then cash in for a prize.

The reward does not always need to be a physical prize. It could be words of praise. Saying things like, "good job kiddo!" or "I am very proud of you!" is in their minds a lot longer than a prize or piece of candy.

If they seem extra talkative or fidgety in class, then give them something to do. Let them draw in class, or while they are waiting. Let them read out loud if they like to talk during class. When kids are fidgety in my office, I let them play with something like play dough while we talk. It helps them greatly. I will play alongside them. This helps us build a relationship.

It takes time to build a relationship with kids. Some kids it takes longer than others. EGR kids may have trouble trusting adults, so they will test you. They will also try to push you away. I had one girl many years ago in my Sunday School class who would sit close to me in class. She did this because her grandma who she lived with was in a wheel chair and she could not always sit close and cuddle with her like she wanted.

If you love kids like Jesus, you most definitely will have kids who cross your path who need to be loved on and given grace. I make sure I tell my church kids I love them often because I know some of them do not hear it like they should.

Put Yourself in Their Shoes…Kids in Crisis

We all have bad days. Kids have bad days too. They get a bad grade, get in a fight with a friend, loose a homework assignment, or something else. Kids get frustrated, deal with it, and move on. What if you as kid totally have the bottom fall out in your life. I am talking, your parents get a divorce, a parent or other significate person dies, you end up in foster care, you are abused by someone you trust, you have a parent who drinks or uses drugs.

Put yourself as an adult, in that child's shoes. Your emotions are all over the place. You are trying to just survive. No one is there to help you. The adults around you are not doing their job, or if they are, they are all over the place too. You start to look around, to see who can help you.

Maybe your teacher can help you, or another family member. Maybe, you go to stay with someone until things calm down. For kids in crisis, life is totally unpredictable. You are not sure who you can trust. You have workers and helpers in and out of your house all the time. You have so many questions that no one can answer.

What do these children need? They need an adult or group of adults they trust who will help them. They need to know their basic needs will be met. They need to know the crisis that is going on is not their fault. They did not cause the problem.

When working with a child or family in crisis, they need a stable person who can remain calm, and help them make decisions. They need to know there are people who will listen and just be there. They need the comfort of knowing who is still there when the dust settles. This is after everyone else has gone home, and life tries to be normal again, or at least a new normal.

It takes children a while to adjust to a new normal. Usually, when scary things happen, there are many changes that happen afterwards, like moving, or a parent working more, or adults making choices that are not helpful or safe.

For some children and families, crisis seems to be a way of life. Some of it, may be because of choices made by other adults like drinking or being jail. These are things children have no control over. When helping try to make sure you are helping and not hindering the problem.

Kids in crisis do have something in common no matter what. They will act out in some way. They have so many emotions going at once and they do not know what to do with them. They will most likely have meltdowns out of nowhere. They will try to control what is going on around them in some way. They may focus on school because, school is their safe place.

They may act out at home because they want things to appear "normal" at school so they let things out at home, or it could flip the other way. Young children may regress developmentally when they are in crisis to things, like having accidents.

Kids may also have nightmares about the crisis or trauma they have endured. This is very common when it is a death of a loved one, or some other big trauma. If this has happened try to reassure them it is just a bad dream. Have a bedtime routine, and stick to it the best you can. I also suggest making "monster spray." This is water in a spray bottle with some lavender oil in it. You can spray it around the room to help them sleep. Lavender is a naturally calming scent.

Kids in crisis need to know there is someone there to help them. They need to know there is still an adult in charge who will be their constant. When working with children in crisis do your best to be this person. Be the safe adult they can come to when they need help or, need to just feel safe.

Change in the Life of a Child

Change is part of life. That is what we tell children. This is a very true statement. Change does not have to be a bad thing. Change can be good and fun. A good change would be getting a pet or having a new sibling.

While some change is good and fun, there are other changes that are scary and hard to understand. Even the change of a new sibling while fun, is scary. A child may ask, "Who will take care of me?" Who will play with me? A child may say they do not want a new brother or sister, but the reality is there is a new baby in the house. For some children, change it is no big deal, for some it seems like the end of the world. Eventually, children adjust and life goes on, as long as they have a loving and supportive network of family and friends to help them adjust to this new phase in life.

Other changes of life may not be good; in fact, they are down-right scary. A change like parents getting a divorce, is a very scary thing for everyone involved. Children know something is wrong. They see their parents fight and argue, sometimes about them. Even infants can sense and feel tension between people. Divorce is a major change. Adults try to bring out the positives in the situation, while a good idea to a certain point can and usually does backfire at some point. Children need to deal with the reality of the situation of the divorce and adults need to help them in the best way possible to work through this change and provide support and care.

Part of any change, good, bad or otherwise is communication. Remember, when going through a big change, children need to be aware of what is happening as long as it is appropriate for their age. Things like a divorce or a death in the family need to be handled carefully. Children do not need to know the same information as adults. This can become a gray area for older children or teens. Use your best judgement as a parent. When in doubt, do not.

If you think it might be too much information, or something that could cause further damage than the initial problem then please do not share this information with your child. For example, telling your child a loved one has died is one thing, going into detail about how they died, or what happened to them can cause great mental damage. A young child does not need to know their loved one committed suicide, for example. This is hard enough for adults to understand, so how do you expect a young child understand.

When a bunch of change happens to a child all at once, it can put your child into an overwhelming overload. They become easily emotional. They may act out, shut down, have melt downs over random things. Change for adults can be hard and stressful, imagine being a young child, and having no control over what is happening to you or those around you.

Children need structure, security, and routine. When those things are disrupted, it can be very hard on a child and their parents. How as a parent, do you help your child through a change? If it is something you are preparing for, like moving, or having a baby then have a plan for your family. Talk with your child about what you as the adults are planning, and who is going to help when the time comes.

What to do in case of something like an emergency? Have a back-up plan. Talk about who to call in case of an emergency, how to dial 9-1-1, calling a family member, a trusted adult, and that people like police, and firemen, are safe people there to help. If you can make a plan and share with your child the plan, it makes something that is scary, a little less scary.

Change is a part of life, but with proper planning and communication change does not need to be so scary. Children are very observant, and very well aware of what is going on around them. When they ask questions, answer just the question. Do not go into detail. That is when things get confusing. Children need support and to know someone they trust is in control. If they know that, then they can feel safe in knowing who is going to help and take care of them.

Children Who Get Left Behind

Celebrating holidays can be very hard for many reasons, especially things like Mother's Day and Father's Day, which for many children and teens is something they just do. They make a gift or card to show their appreciation of what their parent has done for them. They have no problem walking down the card aisle and look at all the nice cards and funny ones and choose a card that best fits their parent. For many children this is the norm. That is wonderful!

There are the other kids who have a parent, or parents who have left them. They have been abandoned by their parent. This abandonment can be emotional, physical, or both. These children are hurting. They hurt because they look around them and see the "normal" kids doing nice things with, and for their parents to honor them on their special day.

Parent abandonment is a very hard thing for children to understand. Even at a very young age children realize what "normal" is. They look around and see that other children have both parents. Older children know what life was like before their parent left. They know the pain first hand of having a parent leave them, and never come back. The reasons are endless, divorce, abuse, jail, a parent being "too busy." Never mind the reason, the fact of the matter is that the parent or parents have left.

The child feels alone. For the lucky ones they have adults who step into their lives who take over that parent role. This could be an aunt, uncle, older sibling, family friend, grandparent, or step parent. This is great, and helps fill a need for that child.

When a parent leaves their child, they leave a big hole and a lot of unanswered questions. "Why did you leave me?" "What did I do?" "Where are you?" "Are you coming back?" "Was I bad?" These questions may never be answered. What these children need to understand is this; it is not your fault! Your parent made a choice to leave. They walked out, and did not give any answers that made any kind of sense.

What does this mean for these children? Will they have problems for the rest of their life because of this? The answer is complicated, but not, all at once. They will be fine, eventually. If they get the proper help to guide them through. They need support. They need understanding. They need room to be hurt and angry. They have reason to be.

These children will feel more insecure. They will be afraid someone else is going to leave them behind. They will have low self-esteem. They will need to have very understanding supports in their lives who will be able to reassure them, "it will be okay." They need someone to say, "I will not leave you." They need to feel safe, because at some point, the one person who was supposed to help them feel safe, left them behind.

As a support person, what can you do to help? For starters, listen to these hurting kids. They probably are not going to trust you right off. They have been hurt by the one person they thought would never hurt them. It may take some time, or a lot of time to build trust. Hang out with these kids. Invite them to your home. It may be that your child has a friend in this situation. Invite them to your home to hang out with you and your family. They need to see what a "normal" family looks like. They need to see what a "normal" family does. Invite them to dinner, to hang out, to church. These kids need to know that you are an adult can be trusted and loves them.

If you have a child in your own family with this issue, make yourself available to them. Help them, hang out with them. Take them fishing. One of the men in my church always says, "Every boy needs an uncle and every girl needs an aunt." They may not be any biological relation to you, but you can still build a lifelong relationship with these kids.

God has put you in the path of that child for a reason. That child needs you. They need to know they are not alone and that there will always be someone there to help them.

Are You My Mother?

Many children have lost their parent in some way or another. Some have parents who have passed away. Some have parents that have just left them all together with no explanation. Some parents are in jail or live far way. No matter how it happened, there is this big hole in the lives of these children. Part of them is missing.

They try to figure out what they did wrong for their parent to leave. Even when a parent passes away, children blame themselves. They try to find ways to cope and handle this vacancy in their lives. Many children seek out a mother or father figure to help fill this hole in their lives.

These children need someone who believes in them. They need to know they are loved and cherished. I see so many kids who seek this out in anyone they can find. They look to step parents, aunts, uncles, family friends, grandparents, a teacher, whoever they can find.

If we are loving kids like Jesus, should not we help fill in these gaps? An elder in my church says, "every boy needs an uncle, every girl needs an aunt." Kids need someone to step in their lives and support them the way a parent would. They need to know they have value and worth. They are not at fault with what happened with their parents.

Kids need to know the love of Jesus. They need to know they are children of God and have a Heavenly Father that loves them more than they could ever imagine. They need examples in their lives of what a loving parent is or does for them.

They are hurting and lost. It is our job, in loving them like Jesus, to point them to the One who can heal their hurts and pains. Not just now, but for the rest of their lives. How do we do this? Through example! We show them the love of Jesus, through our actions.

Loving kids like Jesus can get messy. This is the part that gets messy. These kids are angry, they are hurting, they are vulnerable. Their feelings are raw. They are scared for so many reasons. They will try to push you away. They may try to reject you before you reject them. Why do they do this? It is a way to protect themselves.

Take your time with these hurting children. Let them feel safe with you. It takes time to build a relationship with them. Let them get to know you. They need to feel safe with you. Once this happens, they will seek you out for help and support or to just be with.

I believe when I child loses a parent God provides someone in their lives to fill in that gap. It will not totally take the hurt and pain away, but it does help.

Living separate lives—Children of divorce

When a child comes from a home of divorce, life is automatically more chaotic. There may be very valid reasons for a divorce, but it does not make it any less stressful or hurtful for everyone. There is more back and forth between homes and different places. Sometimes, children do not get to see one parent but only a few times a year.

Children feel torn in many different directions. They love both parents, but they do not like the fighting and the arguing that goes on even after the divorce. They do not understand why everyone cannot just get along. Many times, children blame themselves for mom and dad's divorce. "If I didn't make dad so mad, he would have stayed." "If I would have listened to my mom, she wouldn't yell at dad so much."

Just like in death, divorce is also a grief process. Divorce is a loss. A loss of many things; being "normal," a parent, siblings, parts of the family, pets, belongings, a house, school, friends, holidays, the list can go on for miles. Many times, because parents are busy dealing with their own problems and added responsibilities children feel like they are left on the sidelines to watch.

Children in many cases become very angry at one or both of their parents for the divorce, or in some cases they are mad at themselves. This anger can come out in many ways; outbursts, crying, screaming, yelling, refusing to go to a parent's home, problems at school, drinking, drugs, depression, anxiety, and the list is endless. Children can become angry, because they do not like to go between homes. This could be for a variety of reasons, especially if there is a step parent and or step siblings involved.

Blending a family is not an easy task, and for many families never really happens. The Brady Bunch is only on television. When there is a blended family, things like birthdays and holidays can become very stressful and hard to deal with for children. They may not get to see their parent on holidays or they have to deal with new traditions, and new people to share holidays with. This can all be very overwhelming for a child of divorce. It is not always, "I get two Christmases!"

Children of divorce many times develop anxiety and depression. They have anxiety because in many cases they are trying very hard to please their parents or get attention. They sometimes do not feel like whatever they do is good enough. They may think something like "if I get better grades, or play this sport, my parent will love me more." Then, if for some reason when that does not happen, they become depressed and discouraged.

Many teens turn to peers to help them cope with family problems. In many cases they start to use alcohol or drugs to cope or get attention from their parents. "If I get in enough trouble my parent will have to pay attention to me." Or they start getting in trouble at school to get attention, "if I flunk out of math my dad will have to help me."

So, as parents, to help your child please:

1. Reassure your child regularly, the divorce was not their fault and the problems between mom and dad are not their fault.
2. Make your children your priority. If they do not like the person you are dating ask them why and really listen to what they are saying. They may have valid reasons.
3. Please be very aware not only did the divorce hurt you as the parent but it also hurt your children. Your children may not say how hurt they really are, but just listen and watch.
4. Even after your divorce, remember that your ex-spouse is still your children's parent they love. Please do not say negative things with your children even within earshot or in the house with you. When you have to see the other parent for whatever reason please try not to argue or fight. This just makes the interactions worse.
5. Please do not use your children as a messenger service between you and the other parent.
6. Be aware of your child's feelings, and validate them.
7. Still discipline your child. They need to know that there are still rules and consequences.
8. Even if the other parent does not co-parent with you, still do your best to be consistent (Rules, bed time, school work, friends, etc.).
9. Ask for help. When you are over your head or feeling overwhelmed ask a family member or trusted friend to help you. (Rides for school activities, parenting advice, child care, etc.)
10. And above all, love on your children; they are hurting and confused too!

Children also need a listening ear, and a helpful hand. Show them it is okay to ask for help and to trust others, and when needed, seek a mental health professional to help you and your children through this process.

The Brady Bunch Isn't Real

What is viewed on television is not real. We all know this. The idea that two parents can get married, and everything will blend, and go smooth all the time is so far from the truth. The idea that all the kids involved will just all magically get along with each other is so far from the truth! The reality is when parents remarry there is a lot of baggage that needs to be unpacked before the parents even get married.

Blending a family is no easy job from any side. You are trying to blend two different households into one. Not only are you as the parents combining your stuff, money, and every other part of your life, you are asking your kids to live with people they may or may not like. This is not easy! Your kids did not ask to be put in this situation.

Most of the time, kids are still coping with their parents' divorce. They are grieving and hurting. When a child's parents get a divorce, it is a loss. It is like a death. Then, when you as a parent put them into a situation of remarrying, or moving in with a significate other, they really do not want to be in it most of the time. When a parent gets remarried in a child's mind, it makes permanent their parents are not getting back together. What can you do as a parent?

To begin with, listen to your kids! You are still their parent and you need to be their parent. Make time for them. No matter their age this is not easy for them. They are trying to figure out who is going to be there and help them. There are different rules at each parents' home. This is hard for kids sometimes. They have to adjust each time they come back to you.

Before you remarry, you as the parent need to talk with your children about what is going to happen, and be willing to listen to what they have to say. Try to be open to their feelings, whether they are good or not. Their feelings are theirs to have. Talk to your children about your new spouse's children to see how they feel about them. Are they okay with them or not? Let your kids be honest, because if they try to pretend or fake it, it will not end well!

As a step parent, give your step kids or "bonus kids" time to get to know you. This for some children could take a while. They may never fully accept you, but understand they have their own baggage that comes along with them. They are hurting, and probably very confused. Do not try to take the place of their parent. This will backfire on you! If you try, you will hear something like, "you are not my mom!" or "You can't tell me what to do!" Every kid with a step parent has at least thought it, if not actually said it aloud at least once, most of the time they have said it multiple times, and to a certain point they are right.

You are forming a new family, so try to help everyone feel included. How is this done? Well, family activities, dinner, movies, game night, vacations, hang out nights, you get the idea. It is not a magic cure, but it is a start. Help the "bonus kids" from either side feel included in family activities. Know that there will be some rebellion from your kids, and your spouse's kids. This is normal. Do not be afraid to seek professional help. Learn to communicate as a family. Try to make sure the kids get one on one time with their parent so they have a chance to connect and talk if they need.

Realize as a step parent it is hard for kids to accept you as an authority figure. Let their parent discipline their child as much as possible. Let the parent establish rules with you. Do not do it alone as the step parent. For some kids it may take a while to get used to you, as the step parent being in authority over them. Work out with your spouse how you are going to handle this. Be clear with the kids that together you will make decisions. Kids need to learn the boundaries and expectations of the step parent. This takes time and kids will not usually get it the first time. Try to have patience with them.

Blending a family in real life is hard work. It takes work on a daily basis to get things to fit together. Understand it takes time and it does not have to be perfect. You are not a perfect parent or step parent. Admit when you have made a mistake, and move on. Kids just want to know they are loved and they belong in the family.

Trauma Brings Out the Drama

Childhood trauma is one of the hardest things to deal with as a child or an adult. When I say trauma what do you think of? Maybe abuse, illness, a death, divorce. Trauma is something that is a life altering event of which affects your day to day functioning.

Depending on the person, trauma can affect them very differently. It depends on many variables. What types of supports does the person have? It also depends on the age of the child when the trauma happened. There are stages of child development that are more affected by trauma then others. It also depends on how long the trauma has happened.

What kinds of drama happen? Just about anything. Behavior issues like temper tantrums, acting out, being constantly fearful, learning issues, having a time hard focusing, and so on. Some kids become withdrawn and very quiet. They may hide out in their room, not talk much, not wanting to do the things they used to like to do, and just over all seem bummed out.

Some kids who have experienced trauma have a hard time with boundaries. Some children do not trust adults well, so they are very cautious of who they trust and talk to. This includes hugging and other forms of physical touch. They are scared to be close to adults, because adults have hurt them or not protected them. I always make sure to ask a kid if they want a hug before I hug them. It will take time for a child to trust an adult after they have been hurt. Try not to push them or force them.

Some kids go the other way with boundaries and they have none or very poor boundaries. They talk to whoever they want, and hug and touch people in ways that can be very uncomfortable. They do not understand when you tell them not to do something or that they are making someone uncomfortable. Some kids just need to be taught what boundaries are, and how to have them. This is usually what resolves this issue.

The reason trauma brings out the drama is because someone who has had trauma, they become triggered, and they just react and they go into survival mode. They are trying to protect themselves from being hurt again. It becomes a fight or flight reaction. Kids who do this may just have a meltdown about something that may seem so small, but to them is a really big deal.

How we help someone through this is, very important. Their feelings need to be recognized and validated. Also, letting them sometimes just cry and let their feelings out, is also important. They are hurt and upset, allow them to feel what they feel. Their feelings are not wrong. They are their feelings.

You as the adult or support person feel helpless, because you just want to fix their hurt. You cannot make the hurt go away. You can be supportive and listen when they need to talk. Kids are also learning to regulate their feelings, and so they need to be taught how to do this in a healthy way.

Also, part of the drama can be parents trying to protect their child from further trauma, by setting boundaries with others who have had a part in the trauma. This can bring stress to you and your child, but understand this is part of dealing with boundaries, and protecting a vulnerable person. As the parent it is your job to keep your child safe from harm. Part of that protection. is from mental and emotional harm.

Parents and other adults just want to protect their child who has experienced trauma. They want to make sure that their child is not hurt like that again. While this is a good idea and can be done, also remember, you cannot protect your child from everything. If your child has experienced trauma please make sure that you connect them with a child therapist who can help them deal with the trauma now, so hopefully by the time, they are adults the trauma and triggers are much less.

War Wounds

I have had scars on my body since I was a baby. I have five to exact. You see, I had open heart surgery when I was only ten days old. Right after I was born, I was flown to U of M hospital in Ann Arbor, Michigan. The scars I have are not just little scars either. They are big and noticeable. From the time I was young I was teased and picked on for these scars. Why would someone do that? Because I was different. Yes, I would hide my scars the best I could. I was VERY aware of them. Kids would say some of the stupidest and hurtful things to me about my scars. Yes, it hurt my feelings. It did not stop me though.

Those scars were proof. Proof of what? Proof that I survived!! God healed me! I came to the point that I no longer cared about those scars, because it was proof to me that I made it! I was born a very sick baby and God healed me from that!

When I hear of kids being picked on for having scars or looking "different" because of some sort of illness or disability it breaks my heart! They do not have control over things like that! We are all different! Do not look at those scars as ugly or gross! Look at them as war wounds!

Some scars are not physical. Some are emotional or mental. Some are not easy to see. They come out in ways that show hurt and pain. They show the pain of being bullied. They show the pain of not feeling loved or valued. When I talk to kids about these big hurts, we talk about the time it takes to heal from that pain. You cannot put a band aid on a bullet wound, and expect it to heal right.

These kinds of scars are just as hurtful. They can show as depression, anxiety, anger, and so on. We have all had traumatic events in our lives whether as adults or children. Some of these traumas can last a life time.

Just like having open heart surgery, healing our inside hurts can be a long, involved healing process. It is painful. There are days you want to give up. There are days it hurts so bad you cannot get out of bed. There are days that no matter how hard you try you feel angry or down.

Do not be afraid to reach out for help. Ask for help from professionals, trusted friends and family. Set your boundaries. Know your limits. You can have an active role in helping yourself heal. Just like going to physically therapy after a surgery or accident.

These hurts need a different kind of doctor. They need the Great Physician! They need Jesus. Jesus will not only help heal you from the inside out, but then help you fight your battles! Jesus had war wounds. He went to war for us and He won! There are all kinds of examples in the Bible of Jesus healing the sick and hurt. If you let Jesus help you, He can heal you too!

Chapter 5—Friendship

Will You Be My Friend?

We all want friends. We all want to be liked. What qualities do you look for in a friend? What qualities do you teach your children about having healthy friends? I ask these things to the children I work with all the time. Some of their answers are cute and sweet, like they share or they are nice. Awe, how cute right? While these things are very true and basic, we need to look beyond the basic.

For many of us, the friendships we make early in life can carry on for many years. Why is this? Well, because you find friends who meet your needs and you meet their needs. Friendship, like any relationship, it is a two-way street. It is a give and take, if you are always giving or always taking eventually the friendship will die out. This is true no matter the age. If you are a five-year-old little kid and your "friend" is always taking your things, will you still be there friend? Most likely you will not be.

If you are a teen and your friend is always getting you in trouble, or being a bully, will you continue this friendship? If you are a smart kid, most likely you would not. Parents are there to guide and direct who makes a good or healthy friend for us. They may point out sometimes when someone who a kid believes is their friend, keeps hurting their feelings or getting in trouble over and over, or maybe that person is not the best person to be spending time with.

Parents need to be having regular talks with their kids no matter the age, who is a good friend and who is not. What makes a good friend? Well, those basic things, they play nice, they share, they are kind, they listen, and they respect you as a person and accept you for who you are.

Parents, do you have rules about when, where, and to who's house your child goes to? I hope the answer is yes. When I was growing up my mom had to know who the family was, where I was going, and when I would be home. I also had to check in with her regularly. My mom had to know my friend's parents and if there would be an adult at home. Did I always like her rules? No, but I tell you what those rules kept me out of trouble!

Yes, I know kids do not like rules. Sometimes as a parent you want to be your child's friend, but you cannot be at least when they are young. You need to be their parent and set limits and boundaries. They need to know what is acceptable and what is not. It is okay to tell your child "no."

The other part of your job as a parent, is to model good relationships. Your children are watching you and how you handle your friendships. They watch when you gossip about a friend or say something rude about a friend behind their back. Kids are WAY more aware of things than parents realize. They hear your phone conversations. They hear you talking in the next room. Kids have this magic way of knowing when their parent is on the phone and they can really hear you then!

Also, parents need to give their child opportunities to make good friends. Many of my true friends I had were from church. The reason, was because my mom knew the families. We were all family friends and so therefore my mom knew what they stood for and that I would be safe with that family if I went with them.

When having these talks with kids about friendship, also talk about their side of the friendship. When they come to you and tell you that someone is mad at them, talk to them about why they think that person is mad at them. Maybe your kid messed up and hurt their friend's feelings? Maybe your child was the mean one? Help your child learn from the mistake and try to make it right. Maybe, they need to go apologize for their actions. It is okay to mess up, we are all human. It is having the ability to say that you are sorry and truly meaning it.

Yes, we all know how kid friendships go, one minute they are best friends and the next they are not. One of the things of any relationship is to know that maybe being around your best friend all the time is not the healthiest thing either. Sometimes, it is best to go play with another friend for a little while. If you are truly friends it will be okay.

Now, we all have heard kids say to one another, "if you are friends with her, I won't be friends with you!" How do we help kids handle that one? Well, part of it is that it is not okay for one person to control who your child is friends with. If they are truly a friend it will not matter who they hang out with.

Yes, this hurts greatly that your child's friend is trying to control who their friends are. Then as a parent, teach your child to stand up not only for themselves, but their friend too. I know of times where a child tries to befriend a kid that is not so popular, and the child gets bullied in the process. Hopefully, this child is strong enough within themselves they can stand up for what is right.

Yes, kids can be so cruel! But, hopefully with some talking and teaching we can help kids be able to not only pick good friends, but also stand up for the kids who need a friend. It does not matter the quantity of friends, but the quality of friends that counts!

Design a Friend

What kind of friends do your kids pick? Are they kind? Are they a good influence? Does your child behave well when they are around their friends? What is the ideal friend for you child? What qualities does your child want in a friend?

Well, help them design a friend! For starters, is the person kind? Are they willing to share? Does your child play well with them? Do they like your child for who they are or does your child have to change to fit in?

There are so many factors when children pick friends. We as adults want to help them pick friends that are right for them. We want to help kids make friends that will last. Some kids look for what they can get from someone. Some kids want to be friends with someone because they are "popular."

As adults we need to teach children to be friends with kids who may not have friends. Teaching them to love their neighbor. These children may be hard to be friends with. But, in many cases they are the ones who need friends the most. They may be the kid who is "different" or the new kid. These kids need friends just as much as the "popular" kids if not more.

Not only do you want your child to make wise choices in picking friends, but you also want them to be a good friend to someone else. Friendship is a two-way street. Helping your child design their own friend but also helping design the type of friend someone else may need your child to be. How does your child interact with kids who may need extra grace and help? Do they include them or do they make fun of them?

Some schools are starting a "buddy bench." The idea is there is a bench on the playground at your child's school. If someone needs a friend to play with at school they sit on the bench. This shows other kids they need a buddy to play with. The kids go over to the bench and sit and talk to the child looking for a friend. They hopefully can be able to play together and be buddies. The coolest part is that kids came up with this idea!

Children live in a world filled with bullies and mean people. We as adults need to help children find a way to not only help them make good friends but also be a good friend to those around them. Your child may not be friends with everyone, but they need to learn to respect others, hopefully they can influence others to do the same.

Friends for All

Some kids have an easier time making friends then others. Some kids can walk up to any child and say, "do you want to play?" and off they go! While other kids really struggle to even have the confidence to just go into a room with kids they do not know well. They stay to themselves and do not say much to other kids around them.

How do we as parents and caregivers of the kids who struggle help? Well, first off do not force them! This could cause more anxiety then what is already there. Kids who struggle with having friends usually do so because they have self-esteem issues. They are worried they will be hurt or rejected by a peer. Sometimes, it is because they have been bullied or hurt by a close friend. Try to help your child figure out why they struggle with making friends.

Talk to them about what makes a good friend and why. Talk about the traits to look for in a friend. Do they share well? Are they kind? Do they like you for who you are? All these things are important in any friendship. How does your shy kid deal with making friends? It is okay to have a few close good friends. It is about the quality not the quantity of friends that a person has.

When your child or teen has friends make yourself as a parent available and aware of who they are hanging out with. Are they a good influence? Does your child tend to hang out with the "wrong" people? What can you do as a parent to encourage the "right" kinds of friends?

Allow your child to have them to your house. This way you can get to know them as a parent. You can keep on eye and observe any problems that may come up. Your house may be the safe house for the kids to hang out at.

Your child that struggles with making friends also may be introverted. This can make things a little harder for some kids to make friends. Allow your child to figure out who they want to hang out with. Do not force your child to be friends with kids they do not feel comfortable around.

Some things that may make having friends more difficult. For example, if you homeschool your child, if they have some sort of disability like Autism or Asperger's syndrome. Some children are limited on how they meet friends. Help create opportunities for your children to meet other children like them and different from them. Allow them to do things like scouts, church activities, or other community activities.

When they can do these things, it helps boost their self-confidence and learn appropriate social skills like boundaries and sharing.

When helping to guide your children or teens to the "right" friends help them decide what kind of friends they want, and why. You may need to have talks about things like when a peer or a friend hurts them. Talk with them about how they can be a good friend too. What things they may be doing that are hurting their friend and what to do to fix it. When talking about the traits that make a good friend, also help your child apply these traits to themselves.

Everyone needs friends. Help your child and teen pick the ones who are positive in their lives. Also help our child and teen be the positive friend in the life of someone else. Some kids are just lonely and do not know how to be friends. Let your child or teen be that right friend for a lonely child.

The New Kid on the Block

Is your child starting at a new school? Are they the new kid? You always hear horror stories of the new kid's first day of school. They have no one to sit with at lunch. They do not know anyone. They have no one to play with at recess. Maybe they get picked on because they wear the wrong thing.

These things can cause great stress on you and your child. As a parent, you want your child to succeed. You want your child to fit in and have good friends. These things come to mind as your child goes into their new school for the first time.

To help with this transition you may suggest to your child, find a friendly face. Be friendly and kind. These things help, but it takes lots of courage to be the new kid. As the new kid, you look at a sea of faces none of which are familiar. If you are lucky, there may be one or two kids you know, but it can be hard to fit in right away. No matter what, it can be very scary to go to a school where you do not know anyone.

Your child will make it through the day. Things will be okay. They will make friends. As a parent, be there, listen to your child. Help them figure out ways to make friends, and do well in their school. Meet with their new teacher. Get to know some of the other parents in your child's class. Allow your child to be in after school activities to help meet new friends.

If your child is transitioning from being homeschooled to public school many of the same things apply. Hopefully, your child will know some of the kids in their school from things like church or youth group or some other non-school activity. This will help your child's transition into public school.

Help your child the best you can. Some things will not be within your control or your child's control. It will be okay. Help your child be flexible. Remember, there is a period of adjustment and understand your child may have some different behaviors until they adjust to their new school.

Kids usually adjust faster than adults think they well. Just give it time.

What about me?

Your child comes home crying. You ask what is wrong. "Everyone was invited but me, mom. Why?!! What is wrong with me?" Your child's classmate has passed out invites for a party and your child was left out, and they are heartbroken. What do you do as a parent? Do you call the classmate's parent? Do you talk to the teacher? How do you handle this?

We have all felt left out from time to time. This is a life lesson all kids need to learn at some point. For some kids, it is harder than others. Kids do not understand why they are not invited; they just feel hurt when they are left out. How do you as a parent help them get through these painful moments?

Talk to your child to see what they want you to do. Maybe, they do not want to be embarrassed by you intervening. Find out who the child is. Maybe, this child is not a friend to your child or they may even be a bully. Maybe, there were only so many kids who could be invited for whatever reason. Try not to take it personally. In most cases, there is some very valid reason for your child not being invited.

Then there is the idea that maybe the child who is having the party is not really a friend of your child. Maybe, that is not a bad thing! Maybe, this child is not a nice child and it might be best if your child is not around them.

Help your child understand that they may feel left out but, in most cases, it is not something done to be hurtful. There is probably a very good reason that has nothing to do with them. Help your child understand the possible reasons as to why they were not invited. Comfort your child and validate their feelings. Help your child understand it is not about them and to try not to take it personal.

When your child plans to have friends over or has a party take a look at who they invite and why. Does your child feel comfortable having friends at your home? Why or why not? Take a look to see what you can do as a parent to support your child in having friends over to play or for a party. If there are things that need to change then do your best to do so.

Also, be aware of who you invite to your child's parties. Are they really a friend of your child's or are they someone who is mean to your child? Remember, when your child has a friend over to your home, they are letting down their guard to that child. You are welcoming someone into your child's safe space. Inviting a child into your home who is a bully to your child may not be a good idea.

The day of the party they were not invited to may be a good day to have a party of your own or plan some other fun thing to do to occupy your child. This will hopefully help them not think or worry about the party they were not invited to. Go out to lunch, let them have a friend over, go do something fun!

We all want to feel included and fit in with our peers whether you are a child or an adult or somewhere in between. Helping your child have solid friendships and feel included is a hard job. Sometimes there are hurt feelings and broken relationships that come along the way. The trick is to be able to move beyond it and find out who your real friends are. This is something that will help them as they grown up and face bigger issues of peer pressure.

Sticks and Stones

We have all heard the phrase, "sticks and stones may break my bones, but words will never hurt me!" Boy is this so wrong! Words do hurt! There is not physical mark to see, but there are mental and emotional bruises to be seen! "Bullying" is the hot topic in schools and has been for a while.

When we hear the word "bully" it can be seen in so many ways. A bully is someone who tries to make themselves feel better by putting someone else down either physically or mentally. They find something wrong with someone and they pick on that person's weakness until their victim cannot take it anymore. When someone gets to that point that they cannot take it anymore they do all kinds of things to make the bullying stop. They may push or hit back, go find help, stuff their feelings, pull inward to prevent further hurt, or they in some extreme cases they hurt themselves or, someone else, or even commit suicide.

How do we as helpers or trusted adults help children when they are being bullied? That can be answered in so many ways. Some people say for the child to stand up for themselves. For some kids, this is very hard, because their self-esteem is low and they are afraid. We as therapists work on building their self-esteem and help the client develop a support network.

Some say for the child to walk away. Yes, we do not want to start throwing punches because, then the child who by all rights is trying to defend themselves gets into trouble. The child can hopefully identify "helpers" for when these situations arise, they can go to and get the help they need to make the bullying stop. That sounds good in theory and sometimes works, but most bullies are aware of this because the first couple of times the bully gets in trouble, so they become sneakier in their tactics of bullying. Then the victim can be labeled as a "tattle tale."

We also do not want the victim to turn into a bully because they become angry and their way of handling is finding someone else weaker to pick on and bully. Beginning to see the cycle here?

So, now what?

We are forgetting part of the equation here, the bully. In most cases bullies become bullies because they themselves are being bullied or hurt in some way. It may be by another child, an adult, parent, teacher, older sibling, you get the idea. What needs to happen, is we as adults need to step back and look at the whole picture. Why is this child (the bully) acting this way? Why is the child (the victim) being targeted? Once we as trusted adults have a handle on that, we can hopefully really help both or all children involved in the bullying.

Also, remember with technology and social media, now bullying does not end when the child or teen comes home to where they think they are safe. Nope, they turn on their computer or get a text and the bullying continues! It does not go away! We as trusted adults need to help children and teens by monitoring their online use, and their cell phones to see what is happening. It is our job as trusted adults to try to know what is happening and be aware of the signs of bullying.

These signs might include, lower grades, irritability, anxiety, depression, withdrawing from friends and family, not wanting to go to school, as well as many more. If you see any of these signs ask your student or their teacher if something is going on. Kids will talk if you as a trusted adult will listen.

And as my Sunday School kids would say, "pray for the bullies to not be bullies!"

Mean Girls

When we hear the words "mean girls" we think of some snotty girl, who is so mean and seems to just get away with it. Girls of all ages get bullied everyday day. They get called names, all kinds of names, stupid, ugly, dumb, slut, whore, you get the idea. One of the problems is technology. Facebook, Twitter, Instagram, Snapchat, all play a part in this. The bully does not give up. They post things online and say things in person, or they get their target's phone number and start texting. The girl being bullied cannot escape. They are even told things like "do everyone a favor and just die."

Another problem is that kids do not seem to respect others. They are being taught either by word or example, is being mean is the only way to get things they want. This applies in many situations, with kids and teens. They want something, so they just take it or talk someone into giving it to them. If they hear the word "no" their world comes to an end!

Girls can be very cruel to each other. They play games like "if your friends with Suzy, you are not my friend." Or, "I liked Johnny first, you can't have him." They say things like, "If you don't do this, we can't be friends." They try to manipulate the situation to get what they want. They do not care if they hurt someone in the process.

Girls play these types of games from the time they are young. They become mean and talk badly about others. Or they say things like "I don't want to be your friend anymore." Then the next day they are friends again. This is normal relationships with girls but, what is not normal are girls who are constantly saying these things, or are trying to tell other girls it is okay to lie or other things that they know they should not do.

They tell the girls who want to be friends with them it is okay to lie, steal, and cheat in order to get what you want. They have learned this is how to get their needs met. Then, they tell other girls to do the same. This is not okay for kids to do.

What can parents do to help? Well, first be aware of who your daughter is friends with. Know these friends well. Know who their parents are. Talk to your daughter from an early age about what is appropriate in friendships. Help these girls know they have value and worth, and to not just be friends with someone just because they are popular.

Girls with self-esteem issues are an easy target. The girls who are the bullies are aware of which girls they can target and try to control. Help your daughter feel good about who they are, no matter what someone else may tell them. I know this is a big job! Girls today are just bombarded with all kinds of views of what is considered beautiful, and if someone does not fit that mold then there is something wrong with them and some girls will do whatever it takes to fit in.

Help your daughter have a healthy view of who she is. Help her see beyond the mirror and into herself. There is more to a beautiful girl then looks. Beauty is on the inside, intelligence, well rounded interests, self-confidence. These are things that make a girl beautiful.

Now, what to do about those bullies who do not seem to stop? For starters teach your daughter it is okay to stand up for herself. Teach them to use their voice. They can tell the girl or girls who are bullying them to stop. They can say things like they do not want to be friends with them anymore and truly mean it. Teach your daughter to have boundaries in her relationships, all relationships.

The girls who bully need to know that this is not an okay thing to do. They need to understand that hurting others is not something young ladies do to each other. Also, keep in mind that most likely that girl, who is bullying others, probably has someone in her life who is bullying her. This does not make it okay, mind you, but the truth of the matter is that these girls get it from somewhere.

Our girls listen more than you think they do. They are aware of how their moms and other adult women she is around interact with others. She will see what these adults do and think that is okay to do, when really it is not. Also, women who say, things like, "that is not okay to talk that way to me, or my child," see that standing up for yourself is important, and that you as her parent are there to protect her.

We need to teach our girls that it is not okay to bully or hurt others. We also need to teach them when this happens who they can go to for help and that they need to stand up for themselves. We also need to teach them to love themselves and care for others. Teaching girls their self-worth and value as a preventive cure will go much further in life then teaching girls that it is okay to gossip and bully others.

Love Your Neighbor

Every February fourteenth we think of love. What the world sees as love. The kids give cards to their classmates, there are treats and goodies to be had. This is all well and good, but love needs to be something we practice all year long. We tell kids to love their neighbor, but do we show them how to love their neighbor through our actions? First, do we love kids the way we should? Do we make them a high priority? Are we friendly to them in public? Do we put ourselves in their shoes? Are we helping those kiddos around us who are struggling? Kids have so many hurts that really go unseen or unnoticed.

How do we teach kids to love their neighbor? We lead and live by example! We as adults show them how to love others. Now, I am not talking romantic love. I am talking about showing someone you care for them by the things we do and say. We show them kindness. We love a kid who may seem unlovable. They are the ones who probably need it the most! That one kid who always seems angry, maybe he has a very valid reason for being angry! Maybe his parents are getting a divorce.

We as adults need to listen more and talk or lecture less. Kids sometimes just need to know someone cares about them. Maybe, your kid has had a bad day, or they got in a fight with a friend. Or, your child's friend ends up home alone after school. Why not invite them to hang out at your house until their parents get home?

We take care of our friends and help them when they need. We also help those who are struggling with having friends. Encourage your child to sit with the new kid at lunch, or to play with the kid who does not ever seem to have friends. This is the true act of love. We love and care for someone no matter what they look like or who they are.

There are so many kids and adults who feel so very lonely. Imagine what would happen if we all took time to love on those people. Maybe things like depression and suicide may drop dramatically. Love is not just a feeling it is also an action.

On all the days of the year practice the act of love but also loving those around you. Spread random acts of kindness and get your children involved. Show your kids and others around you they are loved not just on special days, but every day.

Sharing is Caring

From a very early age we start teaching children to share with others. Whether it is siblings, peers, friends, cousins or the neighbor down the street. We teach our kids; it is the sign of being a good friend to share with others. Some kids are better at this than others. Some kids have little to no issue with sharing. Some kids on the other hand really struggle with sharing with others.

Is not this true of adults too? Do not adults have trouble sharing too? How do we help kids share better? Or to just give without expecting anything in return? We teach by example. We teach kids from a young age to share and to give to others. If we are loving kids like Jesus then teaching them to share is essential! Jesus wants us to share about Him!

How do we teach kids to give? We teach having compassion for others. When we go to the store, we encourage kids to pick out a toy for a child in need. We teach them to sort out their toys they do not play with and give them to a local shelter.

We teach them to serve and help others by example. When you volunteer or help out some place take your child with you and give them a job to do. Kids want to be helpful and be of use. Kids need to know their help is valued. It is a good thing to volunteer their time.

I grew up in a small church and my parents did lots of things in the church. My mom would take me with her and I would help her with whatever project she was doing. I began helping in the nursery and with the children's ministry from the time I was about twelve years old. I learned it was important to help others.

If kids are busy helping others, they are less likely to get into trouble. They get involved with a project they like. They find out what they are good at. I learned from an early age that I enjoy working with children. This has carried with me well into adulthood. Also, being a volunteer gets you out of your comfort zone and teaches you new skills. These skills can turn into a job later down the road.

Help your child or teen become involved in some volunteer work whether it is at church, school, or some other community outreach teach your kids the value of helping others with their stuff and their time. This will hopefully carry well into adulthood. Just think if everyone helped everyone? What a world we would have!

Being an Only Can Be Lonely

I grew up an only child. Yes, there were times it was great to have all my toys and stuff to myself. It was nice to not have to share, but there were draw backs too. Being an only child can be a very lonely thing. Having a sibling to play with or do things with was something I missed and still do. I have many friends and cousins to do things with and we treat each other like siblings.

Only children have a stereo type of being selfish, not willing to share, being spoiled, they want their own way, and so on. Only children who are raised like this have many problems as they grow up and become adults. They have a hard time working out issues with peers, they may have a hard time maintaining relationships, they struggle to look beyond themselves. They do not understand why someone may be upset with something they did, and they have no idea how to make it right or what the issue even is.

Now there are some positive things from being an only child. Usually only children are very independent. Only children tend to be more mature then their peers. They also are used to talking with adults, so when they interact with a peer they may struggle with their peer's lack of maturity. Only children tend to be closer to their parents because they are who they spend most of their time with. They can do things on their own and it does not bother them, but on the other side of this is they can also be lonely. It is hard for them to reach out to others.

My parents raised me in a way that I was taught to share and have proper social skills. I have many cousins who are around my age and we were raised like siblings. We would play, fight, and tease each other, but if you messed with one of us, oh man! We have each other's backs. We are still close to this day as adults. We hang out as friends and look forward to spending time together.

As a parent of an only child, how do you help your child not be the "typical" only child? Let them have friends, cousins, and other peers to interact with. Get them involved in activities with their peers. Teach them to be independent. Help them to learn the proper way to resolve conflicts and to not be "bossy." Basically, how to be a good friend. Teach them it is okay to share with others and when it is appropriate to do so.

Sometimes kids want friends so bad that they are willing to give things away to make sure they have a friend. With the wrong peer this could be a big problem. Only children struggle with being bullied and being bullies both. They can come across as "bossy" and therefore turn their peers away with this behavior. This needs to be corrected too.

Also, allow your kids when they argue with a friend or peer let them try to resolve the problem themselves. This helps them to learn proper peer conflict resolution. This will help them as adults. They also need to work as a team and work with others no matter who they are.

Being an only child is not an easy gig. Sure, there are benefits, but it can still be lonely. Also, try to not put the "typical" stereotypes on an only child. Not all only children are "typical." Many know how to make and maintain proper friendships. Keep this in mind with your child makes friends with an only child.

Chapter 6—Helping Parents

Drop the Bags at the Door

For some parents, part of becoming a better parent is dealing with your own baggage. After all you are human. Things that haunt you from your past. Maybe you were abused, maybe your parents divorced, maybe your parent died or went to jail, or, you just flat up had a poor example of parents growing up.

Whatever happened to you, those things leave scars, hurt and pain. They change how you view the world around you. They affect the way you parent your child. I know parents who were abused as children, and were so traumatized by it, they are scared to discipline their children because they are afraid, they will cross a line.

I know parents who all they do is yell, because that is how they were talked to growing up. Some parents do not know how to be a parent, because their parent died when they were young, or, their parent left them at a young age. They felt abandoned. Some children took care of their parent because their parent was too busy drinking and using drugs to parent them. These children were denied a childhood.

No matter what the issue is, helping these parents need to deal with their baggage. They may need more experienced parents come along side to mentor and help them parent better. Encourage them to take a parenting class, read their Bible, pray, seek help. Maybe, they need a family therapist that can help them deal with their baggage from the past, and help them move forward. Having extra support who can help them and not judge them is key.

Part of not judging them is to help parents understand, no parent or person is perfect, no child is perfect. Giving it your best, admitting when you have messed up, and love your kids no matter what, is what it takes to improve your parenting.

Part of loving kids like Jesus is to love their parents too. The "good" parents are the ones who could use a little extra help. Think of ways you can help a struggling parent around you. Maybe, a single parent who just needs a listening ear. Maybe, someone who has a special needs child and just feels overwhelmed. Maybe, forming a play group in your home for young moms who may be lonely and need friends.

There may be a single mom of a little boy, who needs a role model in their life to teach him how to be a man. Take them fishing, to get ice cream, to play with them and show them what it means to be a godly man. An elder in my church who has set up a men's ministry says, "every boy needs and uncle, and every man can be a boy."

Look around you to see what you can do for these parents, who need a little extra help and grace to make life better for them and their children. This helps break so many patterns of abuse, and neglect. Plus, it is loving kids like Jesus.

Parenting Again...When Grandparents are Raising Their Grandchildren

Over the river and through the woods to grandmother's house we go, to live.

When someone says they are going to grandma's house, we think going to grandma and grandpa's house for a visit. Grandkids stay for a while and visit, play, do something special and then go home. For many children, and their grandparents this is not the case. They have moved in to grandma and grandpa's house if not full time, at least part time, and the reasons as to why are endless. It could be financial, death of one or both parents, divorce of parents, drug and alcohol use by parents, children were removed by Child Protective Services (CPS), and the list goes on and on.

This is becoming a bigger trend. Grandparents take in their grandchildren because they do not want them to be raised by strangers, or in the foster care system. What does this all mean? These kids have had something major go on in their lives to warrant this need. For many, it is some kind of traumatic event, so, not only are they children, but they are hurting children. The grandparents are also hurting and stressed because most likely it was their adult child who caused the problem or has passed away.

In day to day life, this means grandparents have to learn to communicate in a new way, like texting and social media. They have to deal with many types of appointments, to help their grandchildren recover and be as "normal" as possible. Grandparents have to learn this new way of parenting that for some may be very different from when they raised their children. They learn new ways to discipline their grandchildren, because in many cases things like spanking does not work, and is not acceptable for places like CPS. They also have to deal with school things like parent teacher conferences, Individual Education Plans (IEPs), grades, peers, and on and on.

For grandparents it is also a financial issue. Who helps pay for the needs of these children? Yes, there are things and funding which can help, but for the most part the grandparents are living on a limited income. Grandparents also lose their freedom of being able to do things in their retirement like, travel. They love their grandchildren or they would not be doing what they are doing, but there are major sacrifices!

Also, with grandparents there is also the risk of more health issues. For example, who cares for the children if grandpa has a heart attack or some other health issue? All of these things are big factors for grandparents who are raising their grandchildren.

Children are dealing with a whole host of issues. They are dealing with the loss of one or both of their parents, for whatever the reason, living with grandparents who they may know well or they may not. Because they do not feel "normal," they sometimes try to hide the fact they live with their grandparents from their peers. What these children need to understand is there are many more children like them who live with their grandparents so, therefore it is "normal."

How can we help these parenting grandparents? Reach out, offer support, invite them and their grandchildren to church, or to dinner, be a listening ear to the grandparents and the grandchildren, offer to babysit, so grandpa and grandma can have a break because most likely, they do not allow just anyone to take care of their grandchildren. But most of all have compassion! These families are hurting and are struggling with many things that we may not be aware of.

Dear Moms…Take a Break, It's OK!

Learn to take a break! Yes, that is right, you heard what I said. Take time for YOU! Take care of YOU! Yes, your kids need you. They need things from you, but you need you too. I know this is easier said than done, especially single moms. Also, I know when you try to plan this for yourself something ALWAYS happens. Learn to take a break for yourself and not feel guilty.

Why should you take time for you? You are a caregiver. Caregivers need a break too. If care givers do not get breaks, they will not be able to care for others for very long. Your job never ends! You are on call 24/7. How do you balance work and home? How do you care for your kids and your family? One step at a time, but sometimes you need to take a break.

How do I take a break? Ask for help, talk with your husband, or support network. Try to schedule time for yourself. Make a plan, and stick to it. What do you do? Well, take a nap, soak in the tub, run errands by yourself. Do something for YOURSELF! Even if it is a few minutes in your day. The dishes can wait. Your kids twenty years from now are not going to say, "Man, my mom could really clean those dishes!" No, they are going to remember the time you spent with them, and you took care of you. Your kids will notice!

If you can get into the routine of taking care of yourself you will feel so much better as a person, a mother, a wife, an employee, a daughter. You are trying to juggle so many things at once, if you do not set a few things down for a little bit you will be overwhelmed, overworked, and stressed out! And "when momma ain't happy, no one happy!"

Also, learn your limits. Learn to say no! It is okay to say no to someone or something, and not feel bad about it. Set your priorities and stick to them. What is important to you? Your kids, family, job, God? Stick to those things, and everything else will fall into place. You do not have to be super mom! She does not exist! No one is perfect! Not even moms!

Learn to take time for yourself and not only will you feel better, but so will your kids and your family! Talk with your other mom friends to set up a way you can help each other out and be supports for each other, both physically and emotionally. No mom can do this job alone! Get yourself some mom friends and stick together!

Busy Little Learners

Letters, numbers, shape, colors, animals, these all seem to be basic learning concepts, right? We all learned them somewhere. Who taught you? A parent? A grandparent? A teacher? Early childhood is prime time for learning. Little minds are constantly busy and moving! Why not use that to their advantage? Helping your little-one learn is one of the most important things you can do as a parent. This can be very overwhelming to some parents.

Where do I start? How do I do this? What if I mess up? First there is room for error. Helping your child learn can be fun for you and them. There are many free or low-cost ways to help your child learn. Children are naturally wanting to learn, so bonus!

How do you start? Having some basic things as part of a routine for them helps. Setting aside time each day or as many as you can. You can do things like read together, do learning activities like puzzles, letters, numbers, and so on. These skills are important at a young age. Make games to help your youngster learn too. I find many fun games and activities on Pinterest. Many of the things I find, can be made out of things around your home, or things that can be purchased cheap at the dollar store or a craft store.

You can even get little bags with these simple activities in to help keep them organized. If you have the space you can create a learning area for your child to help them learn better. They feel like they have a space all for them. This helps prepare them for school by learning to sit for a few minutes at a time. It also helps with learning to listen and follow directions.

It is becoming more and more important for our little ones begin learning at a young age. Also, little ones understand learning is important, and can be fun! Pick activities and games which you feel your child will enjoy. Make several different things so they can have a choice, and switch things around so they do not become bored. You could even have them help you make some of the activities as well.

By also helping your child learn, you get to influence their learning at a very young age. Plus, you as a parent or grandparent can help build your bond between you and your little one. It gives you and your little one a structured time to spend together each day. Then, at some point once they can do the activities on their own, they can do them for themselves. This could potentially help you have a little time to do things you need, because you know your little one is busy doing something. Also, your little one has their self-esteem boosted because they have learned to do something on their own! How cool is that?!

Happy Little Helpers

When should children begin helping with chores and house work? I have been asked this question by many parents. Kids as young as two or three can help do chores or help with things around the house. Yes, I know kids do not "like" to clean, but it is part of learning to be a responsible person. They can learn to clean up after themselves.

The next question is, what chores are appropriate for my child? For small children, they can help with putting toys away, cleaning their room, dusting, making their bed, children of any age can do simple chores. As children get older, they can help with things like washing dishes, loading the dishwasher, helping with meal prep, setting the table, checking the mail, and laundry just to give some ideas.

What if my kid complains about doing chores? There could be a reward system involved. Like they get paid per chore, or a set amount for the week and then extra if chores that are extra are done. What to do if your child complains or refuses to do their chores? Take away their money, they could pay you to do their chore since it is not being done, or they could lose a privilege like electronics, if the refuse to do chores and they do not get it back until the chores are done. There could also be a rule, like no fun stuff like electronics until chores are done.

What about little ones? Make cleaning up a game. See how fast it can get done, or we can go play outside if we clean up, or sing a song to get the clean-up done. Make sure to give some sort of warning a few minutes before cleaning up, so that hopefully it will go smoother.

How many chores should children do in a day or week? Have set chores they are to do every day and also for the week. You could even have a certain day of the week the chore gets done. For example, laundry might be a weekend chore.

Why is it important for children do learn to help around the house? For one, as adults they need to learn to do their own laundry, or cook for themselves, and so on. Also, children need to learn to be responsible for their things. Hopefully, when children learn to help around the house, some of the chores, moms and dads do now, they will be able to have some help, so they are not being all done by one person.

Paying children for doing chores can be a good thing, if done right. It teaches children to work for what they want. When they get paid for the chores, they can spend their own money on things they want like treats or toys. It also teaches them to be responsible with money. If your child wants a more expensive item, it teaches them to save for it. If they spend all their money on junk, then want something more expensive they would need to learn to save for that item.

Children learning to do chores and cleaning up after themselves is part of growing up to be a responsible person. It also teaches them to take care of their own stuff. This is also important to learn as children grow up. So, when mom or dad says pick up your toys then they will understand the value of their belongings, hopefully.

Little People...Big Dreams!

What do you want to be when you grow up? Kids are asked this question all the time. Part of childhood is the act of growing up. We ask kids what do they want to be, but do we as adults actually listen and take them and take them seriously?

Yeah, sure you may get some silly answers, a clown, a cowboy, an artist, and so on. But what makes those ideas silly? Most kids eventually figure out what they want to be. Some kids know from the time they are young they want to work with animals or help people.

Some people including children have a natural gift for things like art or music. Let them go after that. Let them try it out. Please do not tell them that they cannot do something, just because you do not understand it. Ask them why they want to do those things, or how they want to do those things. Let them educate you in order to learn what they think fits them best.

For me personally, I wanted to be a teacher. From a young age I knew I wanted to work with children. I started my college career out as wanting to be a teacher. I then was introduced to counseling and felt God calling me in that direction. I still ended up working with children, just in a different way.

Let kids "research" and check out different types of jobs. Let kids no matter if they are a boy or girl check out jobs in different areas, and help them decide what is right for them. Let them test the waters with different jobs. They could job shadow you, or someone else to get an idea of what different jobs are like. They could also, go visit places like a police station, a fire house, or a hospital for a tour to get an idea of what those places are like.

Let your kids dream big! Do not tell them something cannot be done. If you are unsure if it will be something, they can make a living at, let them make that choice not you. We seem to discourage kids who want to be an actor or an artist, or the latest one is a video game programmer. Why do we do this? You as a parent are concerned if they will make a living at it.

How will your kids know if they do not try? Anything they want is within their reach if they are encouraged and feel supported. Also, if they want to do a vocational job like welding, let them! Those jobs are in high demand and pay well. Not every person is a school person. Some kids struggle with school, and love doing physical labor every day. They work hard, and make an honest living, so why not?

Dreams do come true if you try and put in the work. Who said dreams are easy? They just need to be possible. As a parent or adult, help children make their dreams possible. Be supportive and listen to their choices and ideas. Try not to discourage their ideas.

Kids get enough discouragement in their lives, please do not add to it. Be their cheering section. Not just at a ball game, also in their game of life.

Be Your Child's Voice

As a parent you want to be there for your child. You want to help them and support them in any way you can, but you cannot be there all the time. Do you ever feel like your child is not being heard by someone, or multiple people? Do you see your child struggle to communicate their needs and frustrations?

Part of helping a child is to help them find their voice. I know, I know, they in many ways have found their voice, and sometimes do not know when to stop! In this case, what I mean is this; helping your child be able to in a respectful manner, explain what they need or how they feel. They need help to not be afraid to speak for themselves. This applies to anyone who your child may come in contact with, a teacher, an adult, a peer, friend, or someone else. Help your child have the confidence to speak for themselves.

How is this done? For starters, setting an example. If you as an adult can set a positive example, by listening to your child when they need to be heard, this is a good start. In addition, if you as the adult can set the example, of how to talk about an issue or conflict in a healthy manner, this also helps your child.

Being there when your child needs to talk to someone, they may feel intimidated by is another. If your child needs to talk to a teacher or another adult in authority and they are nervous, be there for them. If you cannot be there physically at least being there emotionally. Help them with the words to say and the way to say it. Help them practice their words. Role play what they may say to the person your child needs to talk to.

Also, be available when things do not go as your child hoped. Help them process what happened and what could have been different. If your child's needs are still not being met, then you as the parent most likely will need to step in and be your child's voice. Speak on behalf of your child. This may need to be done with your child there or not. Ask your child, if they would like you to help them talk to someone who they may not be comfortable talking to.

Go to your child's meetings. Speak up to others who may not understand your child. Help them understand your child's needs, frustrations, and wants. Also, be able to listen to what they say back to you. Remember that teachers and other school professionals, have your child the majority of the day. They may be aware of things you are not.

If your child is too young, then of course you are their voice. Do not be afraid to speak up for your child and what their needs are. Some professionals may look down on parents because they are young, and do not have experience. Do not let this stop you. Many young parents feel intimidated by doctors and other professionals, because they are young and feel judged. If you are a new parent or a young parent, do not be afraid to ask for help. Reach out to other parents who may have gone through something similar.

Being someone's, voice is one of the most important things you can do for someone. It is even more important when it is your child. Teaching your child to use their voice, is one of the best things you can teach a child. But, so is being their voice when they are not able to be. Help your child see that they are important, because someone is willing to stick up for them when they need them to.

As a helping professional, it is my responsibility to teach children to use their voice, as well be their voice when they cannot. Sometimes, this involves advocating for them, with someone as close to them as their parent or another family member. I take this part of my job as very important, and needed. Children need an adult they can trust to speak on their behalf, when they cannot.

Being the one Woman Show of Single Motherhood.

Being a single mom seems to be more common than ever. Single moms struggle through their day, and juggle many different things all at once. They are constantly busy with trying to keep everything going the way it should. There are so many things that are not in your control as a parent. Then adding the fact that you are parenting alone, can make like down right difficult and stressful, or just out right chaos.

Your life feels like a circus and you are the ring master. You are trying to keep everything in control. In one ring you have your job, which for some women is not the best. The next ring you are trying to keep things together at home. Making sure the house work is done and the bills get paid. Of course, this is all on you, because you are the only adult in the situation.

Hopefully, you have some helpful children who are old enough to help you with some of the chores around the house. Your other ring is your children, no matter if you have been a single mom for a short time or many years your kids are your focus. You worry about their education, health, peers, whether you are getting through to them and raising them to be responsible adults. The list seems endless.

It is hard for anyone to reach out for help, but for many single moms it is downright difficult. Single moms may have limited resources, or may not trust very many people. They have a hard time trusting, because of past hurt not only for themselves, but their children too. Also, for many single moms. when they get to the point of having to reach out for help part of them feels like they have failed as a parent, because they have to admit they cannot do it all. Sometimes, single moms cannot do it all, and that is okay.

I spent some time interviewing three single moms, in various stages of being single moms. In my conversations with my three single mom friends, they tell me some consistent things they struggle with. They all agree being both parents to their children is very difficult, and stressful. Two of the moms I talked to have teen boys and they express needing a dad there to help with, "guy stuff" like shaving, dating, and other issues that moms have a hard time relating to. Thankfully, these ladies have men in the lives of their children, who have stepped in to assist when they need the help.

What I have seen with the girls I work with as a therapist; they struggle with feeling accept by men. These girls usually have an uncle, or grandpa, or step dad who can step in and do these things for them, but for many girls it does not feel the same. Single moms see their girls hurting and want to protect them. They also may have been raised by a single mom, and the feelings they had when they were children come back in these situations. To some single moms it feels like they are reliving their childhood all over again, through their children and experiencing the hurt all over again.

Another issue that was brought up, was when having more than one child, spending time one on one with your children, and finding something for the other child to do while you spend time with just one. Kids need that individual attention, and being a single mom, and being able to provide that, can become a big challenge. One of the moms I talked to expressed feeling "guilty" for spending time with one child, while the other may be doing something they really do not want to be doing.

The next issue, that was brought up by all three moms, was protecting their children from getting hurt. In the case of being a single mom, many times it is a matter of protecting your children from their other parent. A mom wants nothing more than keeping their child safe from harm, and many times that harm can come from the child's father. In the conversations I had, I talked to my single mom friends about was trying to keep your child from getting hurt. As a single mom, it is all placed on you to protect your children. Part of this is encouraging your child to be open with you about hurts they may have.

Making decisions for your child on your own, can be one of the most stressful things. What do you do when they are sick or hurt? How do I handle when they misbehave? The moms I talked to struggle with not having another person there to bounce things off from. They miss having someone there to tag team things, and help with these issues. The thing single moms need to remember, is they need to go with their gut, and need to trust their decision-making abilities.

These ladies shared with me some very wise advice, about being single moms. Do not beat yourself up. All parents make mistakes. It will be okay. Take time for yourself, and do not feel guilty about it. Do your best as a parent. There is no perfect parent and there is no perfect child. The dishes will always be there, your kids will not.

Also, as a child therapist, I see children from single parent homes all the time. Please do not be afraid to reach out for help. There are resources out there for when things get hard. There are single mom support groups. There are other single moms who have gone through some of the same things as you have.

 You are not alone. You need to build your support system, with people who can help you, and be a positive asset to your team. You and your children both deserve the best, do not be afraid to ask for the best help when you need it, no matter how many times you need, do not be afraid to reach out for help.

Who is in Your Tribe?

Who is in your tribe? Who do you trust? Who is part of your inner circle of friends? Who can you call in the middle of the night for help? Who can keep you accountable? Who will keep your secrets? Who do you trust with your life, or better yet the lives of your children?

For some people, these questions are easy to answer. They can list off a handful of people who have their backs, no matter what. These are the people you call in case of an emergency. They can give you advice, and guide and direct you, even if it is not what you want to hear. They speak out of love for you.

For some people who is in your tribe may be more difficult. For some there may only be one or two people in their lives who are trustworthy. Their reasons can be a wide variety and can be very valid. They or their children by have been hurt badly by someone close to them. So, to protect themselves they have learned to keep people at a distance.

How do we determine who we let close to us? Some say family, which if you are lucky to have a close family, then that is awesome. I am in that category, I know I can call family members and they will jump in and help, no matter what. If you are blessed like me, that is great! Then we have friends who have become like family. We trust them with a key to our houses, put them on the pick-up list for our kids at school, call in an emergency, and you know that they will be there.

We have these people in our lives, who began as friends, and have proven themselves over and over, they can be trusted and are there to help with anything. They are not fare weather friends. They have been with you through some of the hardest parts of your life. The true test of friendship, is what they do when there is a crisis either in your life, or theirs. Do they try to help, or do they leave or back off when you needed them the most?

How do we as adults help kids figure out who is in their tribe? Are their friends someone you trust as a parent? Do their friends get them in trouble, or do they behave and make your child a better person? How well do they get along? Do they fight all the time, or do they get along, and play well together for the most part? Little arguments and misunderstandings are normal.

What do we do when we let someone into our tribe, and then we find out maybe we should not have? How do we get them out of tribe? There will most likely be an event, or string of events that take place that this friend will show who they really are. An argument, a crisis, boundaries that are repeatedly crossed. That feeling of being used over and over.

You may have to distance yourself from them. This can be a painful process. It is a break up of a relationship. You have invested time, energy, and other resources into this relationship. All kinds of negative feelings come along with this process. You may need to take them off your Facebook. or other social media. You may have an awkward run in someplace public like the store. How do you handle this situation? Do you ignore them? Do you say hello? Do you walk the other way?

We need to be very aware of who we let close to us, and our families. We need to listen to our gut, and be aware of "red flags" that may come up. Try to address issues like boundaries being crossed as they come up. Yes, friends will argue and disagree, but true friends have your back, and your best interests at heart.

What "red flags" are we looking for? Do they cross your boundaries repeatedly? Do they take a lot of your time and energy? Are they someone who takes the fun out of the relationship? Do they just want to complain and not change? Do you feel like you are being used for things like your time, energy, money, out of convivence? If you have answered yes to these questions, then you may have to distance yourself from this person, and yes, these things can apply to your family members as well.

When you look at your tribe, make sure the ones who are in it are there for you, and you are there for them. Friendship is a two-way street. If you enjoy their company, and can spend lots of time with them, and feel like you can trust them then they are safe people for you, but, do not rush this process! Do not let someone in your tribe after only a few times of hanging out together! These kinds of friendships take time to develop.

Has Your Child's 'Tude Turned Rude?

We can all have an attitude from time to time. Why are kids any different? We all have bad days, or things that are bothering us, adults and kids alike. Sometimes we need help to bring ourselves back into reality.

Have you been out in public and your child has said something so rude that you just want to crawl under a rock? What do you do? How do you handle it? You may need to help your child, rephrase something, so it is not so bold or blunt. Kids need to learn to have filters too. This is a matter of redirecting or guiding your child to say something in a kinder way. This needs to have a learning curve involved. before punishment happens.

Then there are times when your child very much has an attitude, and they are being down right rude to you or others, and they know it. How do you handle that without, you know, being rude back? You have thoughts like, "You totally know better than that!"

Yes, your child's attitude needs to be put in check. Yes, there needs to be a talk about saying things in a kind way, and not being rude on purpose. But, also remember, just like we adults, your child may be stressed about something, or someone has been rude to them, and they are acting out.

Have a talk with your child about what may be bothering them. Asking what their day was like. Maybe, there is something going on at school like teasing or bullying. This could very easily cause someone to lash out, or be rude. Maybe, they are stressed about something else?

Now, yes, their attitude needs to be put back into check. They should not be allowed to be rude to someone. Do a little investigative work, and find out what is happening in your child's life, to cause this type of reaction.

Then, there are times when kids get an attitude with you just because you told them "no." This is where you as a parent need to correct the behavior the best you can. Kids know how to push parents' buttons so well; they can even do it in their sleep. This is the type of behavior that needs to be addressed on a regular basis. It is a sign of showing disrespect, that needs to be ended before it becomes a big problem.

It could be helpful to find a good family therapist to help you with this. Someone who is neutral, and who can talk to both parent and child to help work out the issues that are causing the attitude. As a therapist, I have parents tell me all the time, that they can say the exact same thing I did, and their child listens to me, but not them. The difference? I am not their parent. I do not have authority in their lives, and if they hear it from someone else, they realize what they are doing is not right.

Kids and teens will forever have attitudes that will make the most confident parent irritated and embarrassed. The trick is communicating with your child, and trying to get to the bottom of the problem, even if that needs seeking professional help.

Liar, Liar Pants on Fire…

None of us like to be lied to, especially when you are lied to by your child. Now, every kid goes through this phase, at least once in their childhood. Kids lie for many different reasons. First, they want to see if they can get away with something. This could be a big something, or a little something. Second, they lie to try to keep out of trouble. If your child has done something wrong, most of the time, they will try to lie to keep from getting in trouble, or try blaming someone or something else.

Yes, some of this is cute and funny to a point. They may lie about taking a cookie from the cookie jar, or who licked the Oreo filling out of the cookie and put it back. But, what happens when it stops being cute and funny? What if it is a serious thing, like trying to cover up something like stealing or shoplifting? What if it is to cover up that they are being hurt by someone, or, if they have hurt someone else, then what?

Well, lies have a way of coming out eventually. Some kids are really bad liars, honestly, that is what you want as a parent, right? You want your child to be a bad liar, so you catch them and you can punish them for their bad lie, and they learn from it, at least for a while, right?

Now, what to do if your child does not learn from their mistake? What if they are a good liar? Do you trust your kid again? How do you trust your kid again? They have to rebuild trust with you. Also, you need to get to the bottom of why they are lying to begin with. Is there a bigger problem going on? How can you tell your child is lying to you? Does their story change? Do the facts match their story?

When to call your kid out on their lie? Well, as soon as you figure out what they are up to. They need to learn that lying is not something to get into the habit of. It is a bad habit, and it is something they need to understand is wrong. They need to understand, they will be in less trouble if they just come clean, and tell the truth, then to lie about something.

How do you as a parent punish a lying child? It depends on many things, age, and the lie, why they lied, and so on. Do you allow the lie to go on for a while, to see if your child fesses up? This all depends on how you as a parent want to handle it. Is part of punishing your child having them apologizes to the person they lied to? It should be. They need to confess, or acknowledge what they did, and the lie they told. They need to see how lying to others, effects their relationship with that person. I have seen some parents who have their child write out an apology to the person they lied to. I like this idea.

Children need to understand what happens when they lie. People are not so easy to trust someone when they are lied to. I tell kids all the time, I cannot help them if they choose to lie to me. I cannot trust what they are saying is true, if they lie, or what the real problem is. Are they covering up something bad?

Lying is one of those habits that once it starts, is very hard to stop. More and more lies get told in order to cover up the first thing being lied about. As a parent helping to correct this lying habit is very important. Yes, you as a parent need to punish your child for lying. Your child needs to understand there are consequences for lying. Helping your child understand this is very important.

Your child will not get far in life if they lie their way through it. How will they make it through school, get a job, or be trusted by friends or family? If you and your child need help getting to the bottom of why your child feels the need to lie, then it is time to seek professional help. There is a bigger problem in your child's life that needs to be gotten to the bottom of.

Lying is not a good thing for you or your child. You want to be able to trust them and they want to be trusted. So, it needs to be worked out, no matter the age.

Just Stop it Already!

I have been in private practice since 2008. I have worked with children in different ways for many years, before that. Kids tell me all kinds of things. Some are funny, happy, sad, angry, irritating, and every other feeling you can think of.

As kids come to my office for the first time, they may be unsure of me, and that is okay. I am a stranger to them. I take my time to build trust with them. After all, they are coming to me because some other person has hurt them, or life just happens, and they feel broken and hurt.

As we get to know each other, they begin to trust me with their "story." They tell me what is bothering them. What their worries are, or fears, or the things that scare them. They tell me of being physically hurt by an adult who was supposed to protect them. They tell me of the scary fight they witnessed between their parents, and the police coming to arrest a parent. They tell me how many beers or drinks their parent had the night before. Keep in mind, these are CHILDREN!

They have fears they do not even realize they have. They trust very few adults, if any. They may be going hungry because there is not food in the house. They may be homeless because rent did not get paid. These are CHILDREN! These are things children show not have to worry about.

There are times I as a person who loves children, and works with them daily, I just want to look at the adults I talk to, to tell them to just STOP IT!!! Just stop! Stop hurting your child. This is your child. Whether you like it or not, you are responsible for them. They look to you for help, support, and protection.

Now mind you, most of the time the parent or adult I want to yell at is not coming to my office, because they do not see a problem with what they do to their child, or they just want me to "fix" their child. I want to look at them and tell them, you did it! You wonder why your child acts out? Take a look around!

Children deserve to be in a loving, caring, supportive environment. They deserve to be provided for, and have their needs met. Just so we are clear on what I mean by "needs," food, shelter, clothes, education, medical care, and protection.

Children are not something to use, abuse, fight over, manipulate and hurt. Children are a blessing from God. They did not ask to be born. They did not choose parents who would harm them or neglect them. Children are to be treasured and loved not hurt and abused.

Adults, take a look around you. Are your actions causing harm to your child? Do you need to change in order to be a better parent? Do you need to listen to what your child is trying to tell you? If you need help as an adult/parent, then let down your pride and ask! Your child with thank you for it.

If you work with children, or see a child who seems to have lots of "issues" it may be a way to ask for help, and you may just be the person for the job. Take a stand against hurting children and teens. Sometimes, they are too scared to talk, and they need to have someone speak on their behalf.

The kids who come in my office know that they are "my kiddos," and I do the best job I can to help them, and help them feel safe. That is a promise I try very hard to keep!

Say You're Sorry

We as adults try to "make" kids say they are sorry or apologize, when they have said or done something they should not have. While yes kids so need to say they are sorry for their mistakes, and work through making things right, what do we adults do when we have done something wrong, or made a mistake? Do you apologize to your kids? Do you admit when you are wrong?

Kids know when adults mess up. Kids think adults are wrong a lot! Sometimes we are. What do you do when you are wrong? What do you do to fix it? Do you apologize to kids? Isn't that just weird? No, it is not. It is admitting to your mistake. Just like what you want them to do. You admit you lost your cool, or that you could have handled the situation better. I would hope so. We need to practice what we preach.

Like anyone else, kids appreciate honesty, especially from someone they love and trust. They will respect you more if you admit to your mistake and try to make it right. Kids will respect you more as the adult, when you admit you are wrong then if you do not.

Admit and apologize for hurting kids' feelings. They have them too. Talk to them, and be open to what they have to say. Acknowledge how they feel, and why. It may not make sense, but listen. They may have a very valid reason for being upset with you. Talk out the situation with the child. This shows that you value them, and your relationship.

It is not easy to apologize to anyone, including kids. We need to not let our pride get in the way. If we have a tendency of not admitting our mistakes, children are not going to trust you or respect you. They may be afraid of you, and respect you out of fear, but that is not what you want to have happen. Do not be afraid to humble yourself, and set your pride aside when you need. Saying you are sorry to a kid will help your relationship grow stronger.

If we are loving kids like Jesus, we need to admit when we have messed up. Everyone makes mistakes. It is a matter of how you handle it. Do you accept responsibility? We are all humans and mess up from time to time. If we love kids like Jesus, then we need to seek forgiveness when we have messed up, even from kids.

Just Say No Mom and Dad

Growing up we have all heard the phrase "just say no" when it comes to using drugs and alcohol. This is what we continue to tell our kids, as they may be tempted or pressured by friends or peers to use or try alcohol and drugs. This is all well and good for kids and teens, prevention is a huge part of keeping kids and teens from using, but, what about parents?

Some adults seemed to have missed the whole "just say no" speech. They have used since they were growing up, or they have developed a substance abuse issue as adults. They try to justify their actions by saying that it is okay, in some way. Why is it okay for parents and adults to use, but not kids? I am sure many people wonder, that logic, including kids. Drugs and alcohol abuse are just as bad for adults as kids and teens.

How does this affect kids and teens with their parent's relationships? Well, for starters parents are seen as hypocrites, and kids and teens think using is okay, because parents do it. Parents are to lead by example. What kind of example is it for parents to use, and then say to their kids to not use? A very poor one.

When one or both parents use drugs and alcohol, the children in the house suffer. Their basic needs most of the time go unmet. Many parents who have substance abuse problems struggle to find, and keep a job. Things like food, shelter, schooling, clothes, all go to the way side and are replaced by the parent's need to get high.

Many times, children are removed from the parent because of abuse, and or neglect issues. The other thing that happens is children are just flat up abandoned by the parent who uses. The drug or alcohol becomes much more important than the children.

Children are left to other family members to be cared for, because the addiction of drugs and alcohol is so much bigger. Then there are the things that go along with using drugs and alcohol. Adults who may not be the safest are coming in and out of the home, for example. Parents who are using also are usually unstable, and they tend to bounce from living situation, to living situation bringing their kids along for the ride.

This can create all sorts of issues for children. They are exposed to abuse, poverty, unstable home life, poor education, because of lack of involvement from the parent, being homeless, a parent going to jail, and so much more. This is the point where usually Child Protective Services becomes involved, and the children are removed, and placed with a family member or in foster care.

This can open a whole new batch of problems for the children and the parents. Once Child Protective Services becomes involved, it can be very hard for the children and parents. Many times, parents who are using, do not want to change their behavior. Because of this, children end up not being able to go back with their parent. This can cause all kinds of mental health issues for the children involved.

This is where a good child therapist can help. Children need to understand, the choices their parent has made is not the child's fault. For many children, this is hard to understand. They do not understand how drugs and alcohol can be so much more important than them. This is so heartbreaking to watch as someone in a caring profession.

How do we as caring adults try to help these children? Be supportive, listen, let them be angry! They are grieving a loss of a very important relationship. Helping children understand that mom or dad have serious issues, and that they need help, and until mom and dad are ready for help there is not much anyone can do. This is very hard for adults to accept, let alone children. Children of addicts love their parent, but also struggle with the hurt that comes along with being a child of an addict.

If the children are not taken from the parent with the addiction issues, this strange dynamic is created where the children become the caregivers of the parent, and the other children in the home. This can also create all kinds of issues because these children are not allowed to be normal children. They are put in the position of being a caregiver at a very young age. While their peers are out playing and going to dances and ball games, they are home caring for a parent or sibling. Also, these children end up with no rules, and do whatever they want. They are left unsupervised.

The other thing that takes place is teens tend to leave home at an early age, and "couch surf," because they do not want to deal with home life any more. For many teens this creates a whole different set of issues, poverty, dropping out of school, abuse, violence, drugs, sex, and so much more.

I have worked with children of addicts of all ages. I have seen the effects, first hand. To me as a professional it is heartbreaking! How do we help? You may not be able to reach the parent, but try to reach the children. Offer a listening ear, and support. These children need adults in their lives who are stable, and can help them navigate through life to better themselves.

Help!...My Child Needs Help!

Does your child or teen seem to be withdrawn? Are they acting out? Do they seem angry, and you are not sure why, or maybe you do? Has there been changes in their lives, or in the life of your family? Does your child or teen seem to be struggling for no apparent reason? Are your child's friends not the best? Are their school grades dropping?

If you answered yes to any of these questions, or all of them it may be time to seek professional help for your child or teen. I know this is something that is scary for a parent, because you feel helpless, and you want your child to feel "better."

Trying to find the right help can be a challenge. Finding a therapist that can work with you and your child is the first thing. What is the therapist's background? Do they understand, and have experience with children and teens? How often can your child see them? Therapy needs to be consistent for it to be helpful.

Is the therapist's office inviting for children and teens? Some things I do to make my office "kid friendly"? Is it is intently decorated to draw kids in, but it is also to be therapeutic? I have a couch with stuffed animals on it for holding while we talk. My office is set up for play and art therapy. The biggest thing I have is a snack bucket. I fill it with healthy snacks, pretzels, Goldfish crackers, granola bars. It is hard to talk to a hungry kid.

How do you begin your search for a therapist? Ask your child's doctor, talk to the school counselor, ask friends, talk to your pastor. They will have ideas, and places to check out. Call more than one therapist. Ask them questions. This is your child's mental health. It is as important as their physical health. You should feel that your child's therapist makes your child a priority, and your child should feel comfortable with them, because the things they need to talk about is scary. They need to feel they can trust their therapist, and you as a parent need to know your therapist is going to work with you as the parent. If you do not get this feeling, then keep looking. Do not settle for the first person you come across.

Friendly Siblings

We have all heard of frenemies, what about friendly siblings? Every parent wants their children to be close, and be friends in some way. After all you are family, right? For some siblings this is easier said than done. For some it is easy. They have been friends since they time, they were young. Then there are siblings that pretty much do not talk to each other after they leave home.

Creating a loving home for children to grow up in and feel safe even with their siblings is important. Teaching children to treat their siblings like friends is part of this. How do you treat your friends? Do you respect them? Are you kind to them? Everyone does things which are considered mean, or hurtful sometimes. Part of any good relationship is working things out, and moving beyond the issue.

Kids need to know how to properly treat people, including their siblings. Parents need to be aware of things going on between your children. Do not tolerate any bullying behavior. Do not allow rudeness, and mistreatment between siblings while they are in your home. This will hopefully carry over into their adult lives.

Yes, is normal to disagree, and to have arguments in any relationships including siblings. It is not okay to allow siblings to treat each other in rude, or mean ways and get away with it. If it is not handled properly it can lead to resentment, hurt feelings, anger, and broken relationships.

If there seems to be constant conflict between your kids, sit them down and try to get to the bottom of the issue. Maybe, there is something going on between them you are not aware of. Maybe one sibling feels left out, or feels like they are being bossed around by older siblings. Sit back and observe how your children interact with each other.

If we are loving kids like Jesus, then we need to teach them to love others, including their siblings. I see siblings who seem to get along well and love each other easily. Then I see siblings who fight, and argue their whole lives.

I am an only child. I have always wanted siblings. I wished for siblings, even now. I was raised with my cousins around me, and we are all close in age, and we treat each other like siblings. Sure, we argue and get annoyed with each other, but in the end, we are there for each other, and love each other. We were taught to not be mean to each other and to accept each other for what, and who we are.

Loving kids like Jesus is a hard job. Loving your siblings is a hard job too. It is up to parents, and adults to teach kids to love their siblings like Jesus would, as friends.

Chapter 7—Know Your Resources

Know Your Resources

One of the first things I was taught, in one of my ministry classes in Bible college, was to make a community resource list or file. This is something I have done and update regularly. I share my list with others so they have the same resources in the area. This helps when someone calls, and asks for help for things, that is not in your area help expertise.

When I made my list, I would check to make sure I had the information correct, and try to have a connection with someone in the agency I was referring people to. I do not want to make it more frustrating for people in need, by giving information that is not correct.

I use this list almost daily with my clients. I want them to have the resources they need, when they need them. Many times, people come in my office in crisis. They have hit some kind of finical crisis, or personal crisis they need help with. It may be something simple, that can be solved within a few phone calls. It may not be. It may be something that could go on for months, before things settle down.

Whatever the case, knowing your resources will help you and them. You are only one person. You cannot do it all. You need to know who you can reach out to, when you have a client in crisis. Notice I did not say if. It will happen at some point within your job.

The biggest part of knowing your resources, is getting to know your client. Ask them questions, take notes, find out their needs, not only in the moment, but beyond. The first thing they need is Jesus, if they do not have Him in their lives already. But they see their need as something physical. If you can help guide them in getting their physical need met then they are more likely to listen to you talk about Jesus. They will be looking for Jesus in you, and how you treat them. We need to be treating everyone the same. Treating them, with the love of Christ.

In the various ministries and jobs, I have had I could tell you kids' clothes sizes, where they lived, who they lived with, and what needs they had or could have in the near future. I consider this part of the job. I have helped kids and parents with clothes, shoes, food, stuff for school, personal hygiene items, and so much more. This is what God has called me to do. He has provided for the families I have helped.

I know I am not the only one, who has done these things. When it comes to ministering to kids and families sometimes, we need to get creative. Sometimes, we have to step out of our comfort zone. Sometimes, we as helpers need to ask others to join in, and help as well. Most of the time the people who need the help the most, have the hardest time asking.

I know of others who purchased a kid lots of soap and shampoo, because his mom did not have the money to buy it, and he was not showering for school. I know of people who were the "grocery fairy," and would drop off a box of food to someone in need. There are teachers who have students who need basic things, like clothes who will go and purchase, or ask around for clothes for their student.

These are examples of loving kids like Jesus. It is not the kids' fault mom and dad do not, or cannot provide for them. I know many single moms and dads, who do all they can to provide for their children, and still cannot afford things they need. Kids still need warm clothes and coats and food to eat.

This is also true for kids who live in other countries. I know several people, myself included, who sponsor a child. My girl lives in Haiti. She needs an education and basic needs too. I figure, I do not have a child so, I can help who that do. In the states we only see our version of poverty. You truly do not see it in pictures or on television. It is not something you see, until you are there in person watching people go through garbage, just to survive day to day.

If you want to reach beyond the borders of the United States, do your research. Ask others who may sponsor a child, to see what organization they go through. I have been to third world countries and I have seen first hand the poverty and conditions these people live in. I have seen kids living in a trash dump. I have seen kids and families living in a home the size of most American bedrooms with many generations under one roof.

God has called us to help others. We are to give when we have it to give. He wants us to reach out the those in need, in any way we can. I honestly like this part of my job. I love to see smiles on my clients' face, when I am able to help them with something they need.

Keep in Mind you cannot do it all! When we are helpers, we need to set limits and boundaries with people we help. Some rules I follow are; I need to know the person, or family well. Second, I do not ever give someone cash to go get what they need. Instead, I will either go get it for them or I will have them come with me to get what they need. For example, if they need diapers for their baby, I will send them to a baby pantry, or I will find out what kind they need, and go purchase it myself.

My third rule is, do not be afraid to consult with someone else, if you feel the situation is not clear or seems not right. It is better to ere on the side of caution, then to have a problem, or put yourself in danger. Rule four, if you are dropping things off to someone, and you do not know them well, meet in a public place or take someone with you. This is for safety purposes.

You also do not want to set up to be someone who this person you are trying to help comes to you every time they have a need. You are not an agency. This can put you in a bad place, or situation. This is why knowing your area resources can be helpful.

Something I had to learn a long time ago, was not everyone wants to be fixed, or fix their problems. If you seem to be offering suggestions, and help for them to solve their problems themselves, and they do not, this is a red flag! Most people want out of their situation. Notice I said most. Some people do not. They do not know how to live any other way. Those are the people you cannot fix, or save.

If you feel like you are putting more energy, or time into helping someone, then they are in being helped, there is a problem. This is a red flag! I have even in my own experience, had people use their kids to get their needs met. Yes, that is right! I have heard things like, "I am going to get kicked out of my house and my kids and I will be homeless." Yes, this is a sad situation, but you need to take a step back, and see what happened to this adult to get to this point.

As a helping person, it is your first instinct to jump in and help, and save people from them problems. While, yes, that is loving people like Jesus to a point, it truly is not fixing the problem. It is just making the problem worse. How can it make it worse? The problem, then becomes yours too. This person who is getting kicked out of their house had time to deal with the situation better then what they did.

Part of knowing your resources is also knowing your limits, as one person. You can set boundaries with the people you help in a loving and compassionate way, and still be helpful. If you wear yourself out with one person, how can you help the next?

Boundaries you may set, is for example when you stop answering the phone in the evening. In most cases it is something that can wait until tomorrow. Now, there are things that happen that are a true crisis. A death of a loved one, a house fire, and other extreme things. That is something totally different.

Another boundary or limit you may set; is how you help this person or how many times you help them. I know this may seem strange, but some people will take advantage of a kind hearted person. They will run you to the point of exhaustion. That is a path for burn out, and quick!

Self-Care

As much as we love working with kids and adults, we need to take time for ourselves. There is such a thing, as too much of a good thing. You cannot pour from an empty cup. What does self-care look like for you? Is it getting away for a few days? Do you like to sit some place quiet and read? Our self-care should include spending time with God. Reading our Bible, and being with Him.

Part of self-care is setting boundaries. Let your "yes" be yes and your "no" be no. This is scriptural. Jesus did this in His ministry. While He did minister to people, He also did set limits with others, and for Himself. He rested. God told us in scripture many times, to rest our bodies. We are not made to do so much that we are too busy to be with Him. It is okay to say no, even if what someone is asking you to do a "church thing,"

Satan will try to pull your ministry apart. He wants it to fail, or for you to give up. How do we deal with this? Being feed by the Word. When you are in Children's Ministry make sure you get time to sit in "big church" too. Make sure you have time for fellowship with adults. You need to be feed God's word as well.

Over all, make sure your needs are met. Self-care is not always sitting on the couch watching an endless string of movies. It is also making sure you are resting enough, your health is taken care of, you are eating well, and that of course, you are doing things you enjoy. You need to make sure your needs are met too.

The biggest thing I do for self-care is photography. I enjoy it because it gets me outside with my camera taking pictures of God's creation. I have been able to turn it into a side business which helps too. I also hang out with fellow photographers, to learn new things. I also do this because it does not have anything to do with my main job, of counseling.

Self-care could be learning a new hobby or skill. It could be cooking a good meal. It could be just being alone and reading and resting your body. Self-care is not selfish. If you do not practice self-care regularly, you will struggle with your job, and burn out fast.

Self-care for Kids

We therapists like to throw around this word, "self-care." Let's start with what is "self-care?" It is taking proper care of you, as a person. We make sure we are sleeping, eating, exercising, getting our work done on time, and taking time for ourselves. We act like this is just something for adults. Well it is not! Kids need self-care too. What do I mean?

We make sure kids eat healthy, they get outside and run around (cause let's face it, if we do not it is a BAD thing!), they go to bed on time, they go to the doctor when they need, and they do their school work. Along with all the things we teach kids, we need to teach them, mostly by example to take time for themselves. Sometimes, that comes in the form of a "time out" because they are having a rough moment, but we adults take a "time out" too right? We go get coffee, go outside to some fresh air, or find some fun new activity to do.

We as adults need to teach our children, it is necessary to take a break from life and regroup ourselves. It may be "quite time." It may be going outside to play or, learning some new skill or activity. Self-care should be something, that your child enjoys. For some kids, it may need to be more structured, for some, it can just be going outside to play. We have to remember as adults, when kids are playing, they are also learning. They learn social skills; they learn new skills like cooking, sewing, teamwork, and so on.

Self-care helps to teach children, it is okay to take time for yourself and enjoy something, or to just take a break from people, because they have had a rough day at school. They may need some extra cuddle time with a parent. They may need to just vent. It is okay to cry because, they have had a bad day at school or someone has hurt them.

What I encourage the kids that I work with, is to discover what they like to do for fun. Things I usually get are, sports, crafts, riding bikes, video games (in healthy doses), playing outside, just think of the things you did as a kid, and help your child brainstorm what they can do. This will help them when they need some down time, what they can do for themselves. I know kids that are so dependent on being entertained by their parent or sibling, that they do not know how to play by themselves. How are they going to learn to work independently, when they are older? This is a skill that needs to be taught, so why not teach it as a way of self-care?

Some kids naturally just need that time to be alone, and away from others. An adult's job to help them figure out what they can do with their time because, we all know for some kids if they do not have ideas, then they get a little too creative, and then you have a problem or after about five minutes you as the parent may hear your child say, "I'm bored!" We as adults showing them healthy things to do with our down time are a good way to start.

Making it a family activity is a way to do this, or signing them up for a class or team, but also keeping in mind, to not overdue things, to the point that a child has no time at home, because they have so many activities to do. I have heard the family rule, no more than two activities a week, so, for example, may be dance and soccer. This helps keep the family schedule in check, and in control. Part of teaching self-care, is teaching boundaries too. We do not want our kids to think the only way to be happy, is to be busy. That is not at all the case. It is all about balance. It is okay to stay home for the day or the evening, and just relax. That itself is self-care!

Teaching self-care to kids is something that needs to be taught early, and used often. Kids need to learn to take a break for themselves, but also learn to be responsible for themselves. Also, what they need to do for themselves so when they are adults, they can learn to balance life a little better. When life gets a little crazy, and out of control, kids can learn to reel themselves back in.

Self-care is also important when there is some kind of family crisis, or big stressor going on. As the adult watching your child and recognizing the signs of stress in your child, is what is important. Then when they are stressed, helping them to take extra time for them, to again regroup is what is needed. This will hopefully be done effectively, will help your child reduce their stress level.

Learning self-care for children when there is not a crisis going on is best because then they can hopefully shift their gears for when they are feeling stressed, to help them relax better. This will hopefully reduce things like anxiety, and stress to help them when they are feeling upset. This is part of learning self-control and boundaries.

Self-care is important for everyone, including kids and teens. It is a good thing to practice early so it becomes a healthy habit, that lasts a life time. It does not matter what profession, or job you do, everyone has stress. The job of being a kid is not always fun and games, it can be stressful too!

Be Your "Selfie"

Teen girls struggle with who they are, and who they are created to be. They compare themselves to others around them. They want to be "liked." They want to be "popular." But, according to who? To your peers? To your friends? To society? Of course, we all want to fit in somewhere, but what is the cost? Do girls need to sell out and be something they are not?

First, I want all girls out there young, and not so young to know, you have a Heavenly Father who loves you more than you can imagine! You were created in HIS image! And because, God made you in His image, you are not junk! You were created to have a purpose, and to be beautiful just the way you are, inside and out!

God does not care that you wear the latest fashion, or have an expensive purse. What He cares about is your heart. He wants you to be beautiful, on the inside. It does not matter to God if you are a "Girley girl," a "tom boy," or a "Princess." To Him, we are all princesses!

What does this all mean? What it means is, you are God's daughter. You are the daughter of the King, so act like it! Look at yourself and decide to love yourself for who you are flaws, and all. We all have flaws, no one is perfect.

Second, do not look down on someone else! God would NEVER do that to you, so do not dare do it to someone else! No matter how tough you think you are, or how tough you think someone else is, do not treat them like less them one of God's children! Because, that is exactly what they are!

Third, your job as a daughter to the King is to love others. Will this always be easy, no! People are human, and they are broken. They will most likely hurt you at some point. The key is to not let it get you down. Look up, and focus on what God wants from you.

Girls know how to be mean to each other. They fight different than boys, in most cases. They gossip, lie, and do other hurtful things. As a daughter of the King, try not to get yourself into situations where you are tempted to do these things to other girls. Even when a girl may have done something to you first. You need to guard your heart and mind from this behavior. Will it be hard? Absolutely!

You also need to be on guard for girls who try to do these things to you, as well. Be aware of who these girls are, and most likely stay clear of them. These girls could end up causing more hurt and pain. They are not worth trying to be friends with, even if they are part of the "popular" group. Remember, God is the one you need your approval from, not others around you.

Learn to love yourself so you can love others. Be your "selfie!" Look at yourself and others the way God does. With nothing but unconditional love!

133

Happy Family Reunion

In the summer time, it is family time. Summer allows us extra time to spend with our families, and have reunions, camping trips, vacations, time at Grandma's. All of this is fun and exciting. But, how do you set boundaries for your children, with your family?

First, try to keep your child's routine as normal as possible. I know there are fireworks, bonfires, and other late-night activities. Sure, let your child enjoy those activities, but also be flexible. If your child is exhausted then by all means get them into bed! Allow times for quiet time, and down time. Allow you and your child time to rest and have a break. Cousins are fun, but everyone needs a little space to rest. Even if the solution is putting in a movie, and everyone has a quite hour to rest their bodies from all the fun.

Second, do not plan every single moment of your time together. Yes, having things planned like going to the beach, or to the movies is important, check your area for fun trips to do as a family. But, then also just as important is having time for kids to just be kids, and play outside and have "free play." This allows kids to play together if they choose, and bond together with their cousins. When I was growing up some of my favorite memories of me and my cousins were of just playing outside.

Third, let your child choose when they want to give hugs and kisses. If your child says no to a hug or a kiss, respect their choice. It does not mean they do not like the person, it just means they are not in the mood to be touched. These are healthy boundaries. Healthy families will respect this, and allow your child to be themselves.

Fourth, every family has their "drama moments," so just be aware of these. If you do not feel comfortable, and feel like you need to leave, then go with your gut. These may be the family members who may have been drinking a little too much, or like to pick fights, for no apparent reason. You as the parent, need to use your best judgement in knowing when to leave the situation. Yes, someone may be "hurt" because you leave, but they will get over it. You need to do what is best for you and your children.

Family time should be a happy and fun time, but if it is not then, use your best judgement and leave, if for some reason you do not feel safe physically or emotionally. Enjoy your time with your family and build healthy family relationships, that will last a life time.

Is Technology our Friend or Enemy?

Technology is everywhere. We cannot escape it! We are surrounded! How do we help children manage their time in front of a screen? How much time should children be allowed to be in front of a screen? By screen I mean television, video games, smart phones, tablet, IPad, or whatever is next!

Like all things, we need limits. I am saying "we," because adults need these limits just as much as kids. As an adult or parent, we need to set the example. How much time do we adults spend in front of a screen? Yes, many of us use a computer for work, so does that count? How much time do you spend playing games on Facebook, or on your phone? What does this say to the people around you, including your children?

If we do not want children to spend their whole day in front of a screen, then neither should adults. Kids need to see you doing other things, besides sitting in front of a screen. Then you as the adult, need to set limits with kids about how much time they spend in front of a screen. Is it a couple of hours after school? Weekends only? Is it based on behavior? Adults need to set the limit, and then stick to it! Kids will like anything else, push the limit on this. Of course, you would not allow your child to sit and eat candy and junk all day, so why would you allow them to sit and play video games all day? Yes, it is fun, but there are other fun things to do in life.

Technology can be very helpful and useful in education and communication. There are definite positives for things, like internet and Facebook. Students can type papers, do research, play educational games, but, everything in moderation! Kids also need to learn to think outside of the screen!

Kids need to learn to use their imagination! They need to learn to play, not only with others, but to occupy themselves WITHOUT playing video games. They also need to learn that chores, and work are also important, and video games are something that is done for a little bit of time. Also, what time at night is your cut off for playing video games? For some kids, they have problems winding down their minds at night, so playing video games right before bed may not be the best idea.

For some kids, if they were allowed to sit and play video games, they would not do anything else. Often times I hear kids say that they are "bored" if they are not sitting in front of some sort of screen. They have not learned to go beyond, and entertain themselves in other ways. To me this is very sad, because these kids are not using their imagination, their talents, or their intelligence to do something of value. Do not get me wrong, I am sure that on some level video games have some sort of value, but so do other things.

Also, as adults are, we aware of what games our kids are playing? Are they age appropriate? Are they too violent for their minds? Some games are very scary! Also, as adults, what games are being played in front of very impressionable young minds? God tells us to guard our hearts, so we as adults need to not only guard our hearts, but also the children we have been entrusted with. What else is your child or teen doing online, besides playing games? Are they chatting with people you do not know? Are they looking at porn? Are they being lured in by a predator, who wants to harm your child or teen?

We need to take safety measures for our children. We need to monitor who they are friends with on Facebook, Instagram, Snapchat, or any other social media. Also, the computer needs to be out in a common area so their activity can be monitored, and they are being held accountable. Is your child or teen being bullied online? Are their people on Facebook or some other social media site, who is bullying your child for the whole world to see? Who is texting your child or teen? What are they saying to them? Is it safe or not?

Protecting children and teens is our job as adults, and with technology, it can be a challenge. Adults need to educate themselves on technology to better protect their children. They also need be aware of what their child or teen is doing online, and when and for how long. As adults we need to help maintain a child's innocence, as long as possible so they can be kids!

Keep on Readin', Keep on Readin'….

At the beginning of each summer, kids are out of school for a break, we begin to think of how we are going to spend our time. Are we as a family going to hit the beach? Go on a vacation? Go visit family? Read?

Wait, what? Yes, I said read! Part of my summer as a child, was going to the library or bookstore, to pick out my next book I wanted to read. From Little House on the Prairie to Nancy Drew and many others that were my favorites. For me, reading was a way of going to another place and time. I do realize, many children do not feel the same about reading as I did.

For many children, reading is a huge struggle. This is all the more reason children need to read. They need the practice. The more they read the better they will be at reading. It takes practice. Some children are slow readers; some have a learning issue that makes reading hard for them.

How do adults help these kids? For starters, sit down with them to help them read. Read to them, or have them read to you. Just twenty minutes a day will help. This will help them not lose the progress they have made in school, and they may even be able to improve their skills over the summer.

Some may say, this is really hard, why try? In order to do well in school in general, kids need to be able to read well. They have to read for every subject, and be able to understand what they are reading. They need to be able to read directions and follow what they have read.

How do I motivate my child to read? Take time with them, one on one, and read with them. Set aside time every day to read, maybe before bedtime? Some kids may need to work up to reading for twenty minutes a day. They will get there. Do not give up!

Why as a child therapist, am I concerned about if my kiddos read or not? Being confident at something. Having confidence is a big self-esteem booster! Kids who can read well, can do other things well. Kids who may struggle with reading, and finally have that a break through, they feel like a million bucks!

Also, kids who struggle with school are often bullied and picked on because they struggle. They may be depressed and stressed, because of school being a struggle. This causes kids to not want to go to school at all. They see their classmates doing better, and they begin to compare themselves to others around them. I see this all the time with kids.

Some kids who come to me, who have been in foster care, and have not had parents who have not really helped them with learning to read, really struggle with every part of school and life in general. They had parents who did not pay attention to things like school, and learning. It was not a priority. How to help these kids? Well, again help them with playing catch up. Help them boost their skills in reading, so they can be up to grade level.

The bottom line, make reading fun! Reading is a way to escape reality, for a while. It is a way to use your imagination, and learn new things. Children, who can read well, will go far in life! The trick is helping kids find what they like to read about. They need to find what they are interested in. This is where the public library comes in handy, or some online reading system. Find computer games that are educational, yet fun to help kids improve their reading skills.

Set limits on how much time they spend playing video games, or watching TV, and encourage them to read. Let them take that book on a road trip, so they can read in the car. Take their book camping so they can still read before bed. Take your children to the library on a regular basis to get books, and learn what is available to them, at the public library.

I also want to share with professionals, what I have done to help my client kiddos with reading. I set up a small lending library in my office. I was lucky to have wonderful friends donate books to me! I allow my kiddos take up to two books at time. When they are done with their books, they can bring them back and borrow two more.   This helps the kiddo who is struggling, as well as the kiddo who likes to read! Win! Win!

Children need to understand that reading can be fun, and they can succeed as a reader. This is powerful for any child or teen! Have fun during the summer and keep on readin'!

Just Plain Tired

Have you ever been so tired, that you feel like you can sleep for a week? You do not want to deal with people. You just want to go curl up in your room and rest. These are signs of burn out, or compassion fatigue. This happens when we do not take care of ourselves properly. It could result in illness, anxiety, depression, and just being plain tired.

You have been running so hard, and doing too many things. You have not taken a break for yourself. We try to take on too much and do too much. We do not take time for ourselves like we need. This is what is referred to as "self-care."

The term self-care gets thrown around a lot. It has almost turned into a fad statement. What is self-care? Taking care of ourselves. Taking time out of our busy lives, to take care of yourself. Making sure you are getting enough rest, fixing meals that are healthy and not just eating junk food. Self-care is also setting boundaries with others, with your time, and resources. It is going to the doctor when you need to. It may also mean finding a therapist you can talk to about issues you need to deal with.

We need to have a self-care routine that helps us make it through life. Things in my self-care tool box include, photography, writing, reading, having alone time with God, hanging out with friends and family, and other things. I try to mix things up, and try new things when I feel the need.

Taking care of ourselves is something we should not feel guilty about. Jesus did it. He would go, and rest when He was tired or needed time alone. There is nothing wrong with this.

Part of self-care is also looking at the things you and your family are involved in. Do you have too much busyness going on? Do you ever feel like you are at home? God did not design us to just be on the go, all the time. This can be hard to do in a family, when the kids all have different things, they are involved in.

Being in ministry, it is also hard to find time for self-care. People want a part of you, all the time. There never seems to be an end. You are the one who needs to set that boundary. Set your day off, and keep it. Turn your phone off. Take turns with other ministers or elders to give each other a break.

Set up a group of ministers, or others in your field who understand where you are coming from. You can bounce ideas off each other, work together, and help each other out when you need it. Being in ministry can be a very lonely place for many ministers, or others in ministries. Who can you trust when you have an issue to deal with? You feel like you have to be careful what you say, and who you say it to because people like to talk.

You set those boundaries, and have certain people in your life you go to in your times of stress, and need. I explain setting boundaries to kids by imagine having a fence around you. Some things get in and out, a little at a time, and you are in control of the gate of who you let in your fence. Everyone's fence is different, and that is okay. Some people have a fence, and a brick wall. They need to feel safe. Everyone sets boundaries different.

The bottom line is, finding what works for you for self-care. We are all human and need to take time for ourselves. Make time in your day for it. Even if you have to put it in your schedule. Stick to your self-care. In the long run, it will help you more than you could ever imagine.

Made in the USA
Columbia, SC
24 February 2020